WEIRD HENRY BERG

WEIRD HENRY BERG

BY SARAH SARGENT

A YEARLING BOOK

For my mother,
Mary DuPuy Davis,
with love

CONTENTS

WEIRD HENRY BERG

ONE

THE MARVELOUS LIZARD

Henry Berg was a puzzling kid. What made him dance around, throwing spitballs and once even a football in class when Mrs. Curtis was turned to the board? Why did he just guess at the answers to half his math and slap down a number so that when they were going around the room saying how many everybody had wrong, it went,

"Two."

"None."

"Good, Mary!"

"Five."

"One."

"Twenty-three."

and everybody looked around and laughed. Why did he do that, Mrs. Curtis had asked his mother. A boy who obviously *could* do the work. "And look at this!" She'd pulled out a sheet of sentences (the one on products, animals, and tourist attractions in New Zealand—his mother had brought it home and shoved it under his nose that night). "Half of them capital letters, half of them not! He just won't try. He just doesn't care!"

The Question. Henry lay on his bed in the dark, listened to his pet lizard scratching around, and sighed. "You have plenty of ability." The next sentence always. His ability. His brains. "You can do it, Henry. You could be doing really well if you tried." Always during these scenes, Henry just sat. Sometimes he would shrug; mostly he just sat and stared forward, as if he were looking into the distance. People gave up, furious. Stalked off. Left him sitting there, his fingers tingling as if they were asleep, his brain empty and dead feeling. People never left him alone, Henry thought. People were always shoving and pushing and picking at him.

Animals, like his lizard, he liked better. Animals, he felt close to. You could count on them. They didn't fly into a fury, grabbing and shaking you over nothing the way his mother used to. They didn't space themselves out on drugs and stumble around glassy-eyed the way his father used to until he killed himself. An animal had a set pattern and followed it; true, some dogs bit, but if they bit, they always bit. They didn't take your leg off on Thursday and come around lapping your hand on Friday the way his mother did.

In fact, sometimes Henry halfway wished he *were* some other kind of animal—not a human—something simpler that grew up faster, got on its own more quickly. Something that moved in another world completely. Fishing with his grandfather last summer, he'd even started to imagine what it would be like to live like a fish at the bottom of the river. Henry lay on his bed and floated, floated, until he was really down there under the water. Looking up, the world, the sky, wobbled, tilted with the ripples on the surface. Henry felt the ooze of long plants as he passed them, the quiet of all the mud and muck and lumps of jelly things that glowed on the river bottom. Being a fish was resting; it was just being what he was and not worrying about whether anybody was looking at him funny, figuring he was weird. Not listening to stuff from everybody about what he ought to be doing, how he really could be this or that. Henry the fish just floated and just *was*.

A rustling of newspaper on the table next to his head brought him back, up to the surface again, out of his river dream. He was a boy, lying on his bed in Oshkosh, late at night. "Shove it," Henry said. "Everybody can just shove it."

Here in his room, only Vincent was around to hear him, rustling his newspaper in the terrarium. He was nocturnal, an unusual thing in a lizard. Henry switched on the desk light and leaned over the terrarium. Vincent was looking at him—just watching. That was the right way, Henry thought. To be like a lizard, blinking and watching, careful and separate.

Vincent, though nobody would believe it, was not an ordinary pet lizard. If Henry was strange, Vincent was stranger. Henry laughed. "Weird," he said. "You are the weirdest thing in Oshkosh, but nobody has sense enough to know it." He had read them both enough times, but once again Henry picked up the old newspaper clippings his grandfather had given him. They told about Henry's great-grandparents and the discovery of Vincent. The first was dated July 23, 1883; the second, three days later.

ENORMOUS EGG, MARVEL OR HOAX?

Prominent lumberman Adolphous P. Berg today recounted a curious tale to this reporter. A crew from his company, harvesting timber on the shore of Lake Superior, claims to have suddenly come upon a pair of monster lizards, who viciously attacked the men with fang and claw. A battle ensued, from which the men emerged victorious, the monsters having taken flight, disappearing out over the lake. Disappointed at not capturing or killing one of the giant brutes, the men were amazed to discover a pouch or sac, left behind on the spot where the monsters had been sighted.

Made of what appeared to be softened leather, the pouch was adorned with curious embroidery, suggesting magic symbols of some sort, of the kind used by our own savage Indian tribes. Most marvelous of all, inside the pouch was an enormous egg, somewhat larger than a grapefruit, oval in shape and more translucent in hue than a chicken egg. When this reporter observed the egg, resting on a rack in Mr. Berg's front parlor, it was possible to detect shades of delicate reds and greens in a twisted pattern reflected from its surface.

Mr. Berg, upon hearing the tale from his crew

foreman, purchased the egg for an undisclosed sum and intends to have it examined by scientific experts in an effort to determine its origin. Whether to credit the man's story or to consider it some kind of elaborate hoax is an unresolved question which your reporter in all modesty must leave to more expert opinions than his own.

YOLK IS ON MR. BERG, EXPERT DECLARES

A biology professor at the state normal school today pronounced the egg which has had all Oshkosh agog, to be a clever hoax perpetrated on the lumber baron Adolphous P. Berg by his foreman, who subsequently left town.

"The translucent effect of the shell in itself would prevent this egg-shaped object from being a natural phenomenon," Professor Hartley T. Binghamton announced after a close, scientific examination. "The object is obviously of human manufacture."

Upon questioning, Professor Binghamton offered no theory about the manufacture of the object, suggesting that Mr. Berg would need to bring in another authority to determine the exact nature of the substance involved. Mr. Berg appeared today in no mood to pursue the matter further, finding himself the brunt of much good-natured ribbing from fellow Oshkoshians.

Mrs. Berg, pointing out that the red and green pattern faintly visible on the surface of the egg echoes the dominant twisted knot pattern embroidered on the pouch, said she found the object "very pretty" and intends to keep it as a parlor decoration. All talk of monsters, however, has been dropped in the Berg household, and this reporter regrets to inform his readers that Lake Superior will evidently not be able to vie with Loch Ness as a locale for the viewing of monster lizards. Alas.

The clippings were yellow and brittle—Henry's grandfather had gotten them years ago from his mother, who was the Mrs. Berg in the story. "Give him a sense of family. Let him know he didn't just spring out of the air," his grandfather had said to Henry's mother when he gave Henry the egg and the clippings. Being a Berg was a big thing to his grandfather. "You have a name that carries weight in this town, Henry."

The name hadn't done much for his father, had it? Berg the dope fiend. "My father, the dope fiend," Henry said to himself for the three hundredth time probably. He remembered his father: pale, with quiet dark eyes and long brown hair, the color of Henry's. He remembered how his father used to sing to him, and once, climbing a tree, had taken Henry with him, carefully steadying him as they went up. Then, sitting high in a fork in that maple tree, they had looked out at purple hills and brown cornstalks in the field; it was the end of summer. That picture stayed in Henry's head more than any other, more than the bad ones, when his father was acting weird and jumpy. Henry felt sad and happy at once when he thought of that time. Probably he had been three then.

Vincent rustled around again, reacting to the sound of Henry's voice. Pale green with a faint gold shine to him, the color of a grass snake, Vincent had slanted amber-colored eyes and those tiny slits reptiles had for ears. The lizard always listened to him talk, Henry noticed, in a way that struck him as strange. The chameleon he got at a circus once and kept all year until it died from eating mealworm shells never looked around if he talked to it, never noticed Henry unless he was putting bugs in its terrarium.

Vincent even knew his name; Henry had tested him over and over. He would come in and say, "Hi, Vincent." Immediately, the lizard's eyes were on him, expectant. He reacted to other words by stirring around, acting curious, but not the same way he did to his name. "Look here, Vincent," Henry said. "Look at this pouch here. Who made this pouch? Some Indian somewhere?" He held the embroidered bag up close to the terrarium, and Vincent stuck his nose up against the glass, looking at it.

The day Vincent hatched had been the outstanding day in his life so far, Henry thought. That smoke—a sudden puff of reddish smoke had risen from his bureau where the egg was. Henry had leaped up and rushed over, and found no egg at all, and no shell—just Vincent, coming uncurled. Funny, Henry thought, he hadn't been scared. Thinking about it later, he got a little scared. But at the time, standing there astonished, watching Vincent stretch himself, he'd felt great, wonderful. "What a marvelous lizard," he'd thought. *Marvelous*, a weird word he never used. But that was the word he thought then, wanting to take care of this mysterious animal, this wonderful shining lizard hatching out on his bureau before dinner.

"Now don't be tiresome, Henry," his mother had said that night. "And calm down that overactive imagination of yours." She had smiled across at Dr. Ferguson, who was having dinner with them. "You didn't have my permission to get a lizard; this kind of story isn't going to do you a bit of good."

Henry had gotten mad, seeing her look at Ferguson to back her up. Henry hated the way she cared so much what everybody thought. She worried all the time about doing something wrong, not being perfect. He knew why she was like that. All that she'd been through with his father made her scared. And now she was watching Henry, seeing signs that he was turning out weird, too. Henry knew she thought he would never be a normal person. Telling him what to do every minute, watching and picking at him, never in his whole life trusting him for one second.

"Henry," Dr. Ferguson had asked, "are you sure you're giving us the whole story here? Look, if something happened to that egg, if you broke it or something, it's not the end of the world. Everybody makes mistakes once in a while."

His mother gasped. She hadn't thought of that. "*Henry!* You didn't break that egg of Grandad's!" She looked over at Dr. Ferguson. "He'll just die, Jim. That egg has been in the family for almost a hundred years."

"I told you what happened," Henry said. "And that is what happened. You never believe me. I'm just Henry—

what difference do *I* make? What do *I* ever know?" And he had turned around and stalked out, slamming the door to his room.

For the whole week since then his mother had been mad, but trying to act calm, the way she'd learned to in that "parenting" class she was taking at the university. That was where she'd run into Ferguson—he was the big expert on a panel one night. Henry could see she was trying to calm down, to act less mean. He knew he ought to be glad, ought to try to be nicer too. But he couldn't make himself do it. Because how real was all this stuff? Following some kind of script like they were on TV. Maybe next week she would take up tennis and go back to screaming and yelling. Instead of trying to get him to "discuss" it, to say why he'd made up the story. To say he'd broken the egg. To tell her he'd gotten Vincent at the pet shop.

"Henry," she kept saying, "we all make mistakes. I make mistakes, too, but I admit it when I do. I can be supportive, Henry, if you'll just tell me what really happened. I can accept you, Henry, even if you sometimes do things I can't accept. Can't you see the difference?"

"*All right!*" he'd finally yelled last night. "All right! I broke Grandad's egg! The old Berg hundred-year-old egg! I broke it. I bought Vincent at the Pet Bazaar. Are you happy now? Will you leave me alone once in a while now?"

But he'd overdone it. He could see that shine in her eyes that meant she was good and mad, that meant she hated him. She wanted to feel on top all the time, that was it. She had to be the boss. He had to be like some kind of pet—ordered around and grateful for whatever was handed out.

"Look, Henry," she said. "I'm sorry if you think I'm being unfair. But I don't think you should keep that lizard because you didn't tell the truth about it. I know I haven't always been all that perfect myself, and I'm sorry. But we've got to tell the truth to each other, that's all. You can't live with another person and not be able to believe him."

That was the way they had left it. And now, on top of everything else, she had gone to the PTA meeting. All that stuff from Mrs. Curtis about his math and his capital letters and his attitude would put the clincher on Vincent for sure.

"Don't worry about it, Vincent," said Henry, turning off the light and crawling into bed. "Tomorrow you'll go to a new place. But you'll be okay, Vincent. You are my lizard. You are going to stay my lizard."

TWO

A MISSION IN OSHKOSH

That same night while Henry was lying in his room, thinking and talking to Vincent, high in the sky over Oshkosh a dark figure floated. A bat-winged creature, bigger than a man, was circling, gliding above the trees, graceful as the fish in Henry's dream, swimming in the sky above his head. It was Aelf, looking for a place to land.

He wanted to land in town because the house he had to find was there, but he needed a space that was private, that would give him a chance to put on the raincoat he had brought for a disguise, to look at his map and decide where to go. Aelf circled lower and lower, coming in at treetop level before he spotted a vacant lot, cut off from the street by a hedge. It had a tree off at the end of it that would give him a dark spot, away from the streetlight, to get himself ready. It was in the center of town, too. Perfect, he thought with some pride. He banked, came around, and lighted under the tree.

The flight itself had been pleasant, Aelf was thinking, unbuckling the pack he'd strapped to his back, pulling out the enormous raincoat he'd brought to drape himself in. He was nervous, though, afraid that the light from the streetlight would reflect off his skin and give him away at the very start. Being here, a dragon in Oshkosh, he would be something to stare at, to make people scream. Even without dragons to startle them, people jumped and leaped around like bugs, like grasshoppers in the summer grass, Aelf thought. He himself moved to a slower rhythm: usually, in fact, didn't move at all.

Usually he lay along the stone ledges of his cave with the others and blinked his eyes to watch the light flash, hissed a little fire once in awhile to feel the small flames licking around his teeth, to watch the orange plumes dance around his snout. Now, pulling on the coat, softly to himself he muttered a kind of chant:

> Worm-weards, gold-guardians,
> Be beside your brother,
> Hoard-keepers, help and defend
> One far from home, from fire and from friend.

For a minute it brought back the darkness of the caves in Wales, the gold glint of the coins, and the smell of smoke. For a minute it made him feel almost at home.

Aelf wanted to be at home, not here. Dragons liked to

stay apart; not to mix and muddle their lives with people's. And no dragon in Wales was more attached to his cave than Aelf, no dragon was less interested in flapping his wings and visiting the strange town of Oshkosh. Probably, Aelf thought, struggling to button the coat without tangling his claws in the buttonholes, probably that was why the Old One had picked him.

He thought back to the scene in the cave that night. The Old One, Hrothan, sleeping in the cup-like dip in the center of the cave. Awake only when he had to be, when they had to rouse him and ask him what to do. The last time had been nearly a hundred years ago, when this awful Oshkosh business had started. Even to Aelf, there was something dreadful about Hrothan's enormous flanks, puffing in and out in sleep, the folds and layers of dragon flesh coiled in the center of the cave, and, then, when he was awake, the fierce glow suddenly from his eyes and the thin, narrow voice from a long distance, like the trickle of water over stone.

"Send Aelf," he had said. "Send Aelf to find Orm. To bring him back." Then his head had slumped back along his claws, his eyes had closed, and Hrothan was asleep again.

Now that he was here in Oshkosh, Aelf almost wished Hrothan had picked Eadmund or Winnbrod. Left him in peace. But, he thought with some pride, neither of them would have had the sense to come in the middle of the night, to look carefully down at the street below to find an empty space, to get himself wrapped in a disguise right away. Some dragons would just go stomping along, eyes glowing, smoke twirling from their nostrils, never giving a thought to being secret, to keeping out of sight.

Aelf reached into the raincoat pocket for the map and the address where he was to look for Orm. Peering at it and trying to decide where he was and how to get to where Orm was made Aelf's head start to ache and his ears hum. It was true he was smarter than Winnbrod, more careful than Eadmund, but still, no dragon found thinking easy. The darkness under the tree made the map hard to see, besides. Aelf made his eyes glow faintly, just enough to see the lines on the paper he held up in front of his snout.

As soon as his eyes lit up, Aelf heard a rustling off in the hedge by the street. He looked up from the map to see a small brown and white terrier dashing into the lot toward him, its hair all bristled up on end, rumbling and growling. The dog made a sweeping run toward him, veered off, dashed back to the hedge, and then ran toward him again.

Aelf felt disgusted. Dogs. Hanging around people all the time, yapping and zipping around, going nowhere. And this one was a real danger. His noise would attract attention, bring people. Aelf sighed. He would have to take time to kill the dog. He put the map back into his pocket and opened his mouth—snapped his jaws open and shut, open and shut, getting his muscles back in shape after the long flight. He was ready to lunge.

And lunge he did, but just at that moment something else came charging out of the bushes, dashing across the lot, ramming into his legs and throwing him off balance. Instead of sinking into the dog, his teeth bit on air, clacking together as Aelf fell over backward into the tree. Too startled for a minute to think, Aelf sat up, looking to see what in Oshkosh would be hurling itself against a dragon. It was a lady, old for a human. A wiry lady with short gray hair, her glasses knocked crooked in the fall.

Dashing across the lot, Millie had been afraid—terrified, even. But all she could think of, hurling herself straight at the monster, was Jack, her dog. She had to keep Jack away from all those alligator teeth she'd seen flashing in the light. True, she shouldn't have been on the street so late at night, coming out just because Jack wanted to. It was dangerous. Respectable old ladies stayed inside after dark with their doors bolted. She knew that. And she knew she had to watch for the usual dangers—muggers and drunks. But never had she considered meeting a monster, never had she thought of what she'd do if she came upon a flying alligator.

A few minutes before, Millie had been crouching behind the hedge, hardly believing what she had just seen land over by the tree. When the flash from the monster's eyes had gone off, and Jack broke loose and headed straight toward it, Millie had followed without thinking. Rushing blindly after Jack across the lot, she had hurled herself like a Green Bay Packer at the enormous alligator. Now half the wind was knocked out of her, and she was rolling, tangled on the ground, caught in the folds of the creature's raincoat.

"Help," she sputtered out, too breathless to make much noise, "Police! Somebody! Help!"

Aelf pulled his coat out from under her and stood up. That was what he detested about humans. Never made any sense. Came dashing and galloping at you for no reason, even knocked you over, and then blamed you. He felt fury rising, wanted to feel the human's bones snap and crunch under his claws, wanted to see the dog incinerated by one blast of flame from his throat. His eyes glowing red and orange, he felt little wisps of smoke starting to curl out of his nostrils.

"Aelf, Aelf," he told himself, "the Old One. Remember the Old One." Always the Old One had cautioned against crushing humans. When one human was destroyed, others came in flocks and swarms, with lights and noise, searching. It was a danger. Aelf had to be secret, had to hold himself in. Only if there was no other way could he kill a human.

Millie sat up and looked around frantically. Jack had stopped barking; he was crouched at her side, rumbling and gurgling. There was nobody downtown to hear her. She stopped trying to scream and took two deep breaths. Outer space maybe? Could this be some creature from Mars or somewhere? Millie looked up into the sky, for a saucer or more beasts. A few stars and gray mist. Nothing else. Whatever it was, it seemed to be by itself. In Oshkosh? Millie stared at its back, turned away from her, and tried to grasp what was happening.

"Can you talk?" she said finally. "Do you speak English?"

Aelf nearly choked on the insult of it. Some lady in Oshkosh asking if he spoke English. In Britain nobody thought *she* spoke English. Whose language was it? He snorted.

"I speak English," he spat out, teeth clenched. "What else?"

"Will you let us go?" she begged in a quiet voice. "What are you—somebody playing a joke or something?"

"Let you go?" Aelf said, wheeling around, eyes flashing at her. "Who attacked whom? I have a mission in Oshkosh. I make plans. I get here when humans are all supposed to be asleep. I land in an empty space. Then when I am standing, reading my map, you and that dog leap on top of me, knock me to the ground, wrinkle my raincoat. I can assure you, madame, I am playing no joke. I am attempting to attend to my own business."

"Well, you have to admit, you are unusual," Millie blurted out, staring at him now that he was facing her. Blinking twice to clear her head, she looked straight up into his face. His gold eyes shone out like slanted moons and there was a gleam about him like the sequins on her old evening bag. Fern-green, his nose was blunter than an alligator's and ended in large flared nostrils. Wisps of smoke still curled from them.

Aelf snorted again. "Unusual!" She was lucky he was "unusual." If he had been any of the others—Wilfred, Eadgar, Eadmund or Winnbrod—she would have been a pile of bones by now. No dragon wasted time wondering and poking behind things but, luckily for her, Aelf was unusually intelligent for a dragon. Before he blew fire, there was a second he took to think, to remind himself of the Old One and his cautions. Before he raked his claws across a human or crushed a dog or a sheep in his jaws, he weighed what he was doing, to see if it was a good thing. Aelf was here for one reason—to find Orm. If he could talk to this lady, get her to be sensible and stop leaping and twitching and shrieking the way humans did, maybe she could even help him.

"I had no wish to frighten you," he said stiffly. Then, nearly choking on it, Aelf forced himself a step further than he ever thought he would go. "Sorry," he said. A dragon, apologizing to a human. He could hardly believe it. But the mission was important; the Old One had chosen him; whatever he needed to do, Aelf would do. "I am sorry, madame."

Like Aelf, Millie was unusually smart—but she was less cautious, not the sort of person to want today to be just like yesterday. Millie tried new things—voted for the person the paper called a "radical" in the last election, shook garlic salt all over her mashed potatoes when she went to the senior citizens' dinners, walked her dog in the middle of the night. Now her curiosity aroused, her fear subsiding, Millie stared at Aelf. She *had* run into him, knocked him over. He was—whatever else he might be—a stranger in town, a guest. Millie had always despised people who shrank away from anything the least bit different, who never took a chance on anything. She brushed herself off and motioned to Jack, still cowering on his belly and growling.

"My dog and I will be heading home," she said. "You are welcome to join us. Study your map in my living room where you'll have some light."

Aelf's eyes glowed for a sudden second or two. "You are kind," he said. To go to this lady's lair, to get out of sight for a time and make his plans, was more than he had hoped for.

Millie lived in an apartment up over a shoe repair shop in one of the old three-story brick buildings just off Main Street. It was only a block or so away. Aelf picked up his pack, Millie hitched Jack's leash on, and they walked down the deserted street, a strange-looking little parade. Aelf, though he was taller than the tallest basketball player and very powerful, moved with an easy grace, quiet as a flame. Millie hurried along beside him, pulling Jack, who still bristled and rumbled deep in his throat every once in a while. When they got to her building, Millie hurried up the stairs first, then unlocked the door, and gestured for Aelf to enter.

Inside, Aelf looked around uneasily. Walking across the living room, he brushed his raincoat against a lamp and had to grab it before it fell over. Everything was so small and padded and covered with cloth. No stone ledge to lie on. The apartment was full of human smells—floor wax and cabbage and toothpaste. Aelf's nostrils twitched and he wanted to be back outside, smelling the damp night. He looked toward the kitchen and past the bedroom door, scanning the room for any sign of a trap. He saw no guns, smelled no danger. Aelf sighed and sat, where Millie pointed, on her sofa.

His giant shape filled up her living room, suddenly making the familiar space seem strange to Millie. Her sofa groaned under the weight of the enormous lizard. Suppose he suddenly lunged at her? Blew that torch breath of his across the room and set the whole building on fire? "Well, he's here now," she muttered under her breath. "A little late to think of that, Millie Levenson."

Uneasily, they sat and stared at each other. "My name is Millie," she finally said, just to break the silence. "I'm Millie Levenson."

"Aelf," the dragon said. "How do you do?" Sitting here, trying to think, was giving Aelf a headache. He looked at Millie, stared close at her face, trying to guess what she might be thinking. She could help him, if only he could trust her. It was a chance, a risk, but Aelf decided to take it. To him, so far, she seemed less foolish than most humans, telling him her name, giving away her own secrets. That was a sign of friendship, of peace, the giving of names.

"I am a dragon. Here from Wales on a mission. It has to be secret. My presence has to be secret. Will you keep everything to yourself if I explain?"

Millie just looked at him, too astonished to speak. She nodded. Aelf started to talk, to tell her about the Old One and about his reason for sending Aelf to Oshkosh.

"This Orm," Millie said, sitting on the recliner and looking across at Aelf on the couch. "How did you say he came to be born in Oshkosh?" Millie was having trouble following, maybe because it was after 2:00 in the morning. She kept saying to herself, "I'm sitting on this La-Z-Boy recliner in my own front room, leaning on my own pillow with the velvet picture of the Black Hills, talking to a dragon named Aelf." She kept saying it to stop this feeling that she was floating off, like a balloon in the sky.

"When the egg was taken," Aelf explained again, "we decided to wait. If we came, tearing and burning, the shell might be broken and Orm might die. When Grettir and

Hilde flew home from America, and the dragon circle asked what should be done, the Old One said, 'Wait.' So we waited."

"Ninety-five years," Millie said, still amazed. "And an egg, too. Just like a chicken."

"Or a python, or a peacock," Aelf said, somewhat miffed. People were tiresome in the end, he thought, even the nicer ones: narrow, thinking that their own pasty faces, with their silly stubs for noses and those foolish fuzzes of hair hiding the curve of the skull, thinking that these blurred fat faces were somehow beautiful, were somehow the best way to look. He rolled his eyes down, admiring the long green shine of his snout.

"And it all happened because this other dragon, this cousin of yours, Grettir, wanted a trip?"

Aelf sighed. The foolishness of the whole thing. Talking about it was painful, brought it all back. Human beings were tourists. Dragons were not. From his cave, Aelf had seen humans dragging themselves up to the top of a nearby mountain, staring around at everything through binoculars. Trotting back and forth, busy doing nothing that he could see. Until Grettir, no dragon had ever been stirred by any such foolish urge. "He heard of the New World," Aelf said. "So many of your sort were coming to Wales. He overheard talk about America."

"Well, good for him," Millie said. "What's the use of sticking around some smelly cave all your life? See the world." Aelf was starting to get on her nerves with this thing about staying in one place all the time.

"Look at my pillow from Mount Rushmore," she said. "It's beautiful out there. It gives you memories. Gives you something you've done in your life."

"Men seek treasures," Aelf nodded at the pillow. "Dragons keep them. But, it is true, Grettir's wings wanted to beat; he loved the wind across his scales." And Grettir had come to America, Aelf explained to Millie, with his wife Hilde. They had found themselves a landing place in the wilderness, near Lake Superior. They were there, tails trailing in the water, talking of the wonders they'd seen, when the lumbermen attacked. "Grettir and Hilde left Orm—an egg then—in a pouch on the shore. Then they flew away over the lake."

"Were they afraid that if they attacked, Orm would be hurt?"

"That, and also that men would see too much of them. The Old One says men and dragons should stay apart. We don't want to be seen," Aelf said. "That's why I brought this coat," he explained proudly, "for a disguise."

Millie looked at him. He was about eight feet tall and bright green. "It's a good idea," she said gently, having learned by now that Aelf's feelings were not hard to hurt. "Very smart, but maybe you'd better let me help you out a little. Do some of the scouting around in the daytime. If I checked out that address for you, found out something about what's over there, it might be easier."

First thing that might happen, if something like Aelf started walking around the streets of Oshkosh, she thought, was that people would scream and run. They would get the police or somebody with a gun and chase him down.

Millie remembered a deer that had somehow wandered into town a few years ago and then run wild in a panic. It had jumped through a department store window, and was staggering bleeding down the middle of Main Street when somebody had finally caught up to it and shot it. She shuddered and got her mind back to Orm.

"So the lumbermen brought the egg here and sold it to their boss, is that it?"

"Yes," Aelf said, "and it became a treasure in the man's house. On a table in his great hall for everyone to see. We knew then it would be safe, that he would guard it."

"And that address is where the man lived, where the egg was?" Millie asked.

"Yes," Aelf answered. "And where I will go to find Orm. To bring him back."

"But who lives in the house now?" Millie asked.

"The man's son must, surely," Aelf said, surprised. "When a man dies, his son keeps his house, holds his treasures." He looked blankly at Millie, fear stirring. Was the Old One wrong to tell them to wait? Could they have moved Orm away, lost him?

"Those big old houses are mostly apartments now, Aelf," Millie said. "The man's family may have moved to California, Arizona, anywhere. The lumber business is mostly gone from Oshkosh now and the lumber families too." She looked at him, not wanting to upset him too much, but not wanting him to go rushing over to that old house in the middle of the night expecting to find Orm on the front porch waiting for him. Aelf would have to learn that people don't stay put forever the way dragons evidently did.

"But I can ask around, find out for you. You can stay here until we have something definite to go on." Under the table-cloth Jack gave a deep-throated growl. "Quiet, Jack," Millie said. "Come on out from under there. It's time we went to bed. Tomorrow will be soon enough to start looking."

Aelf got up, watching Millie and Jack going into the bedroom. He peered after them, over Millie's shoulder, to make sure they couldn't go out without coming past him. The bedroom had only one door. Aelf sighed and stood by the window, looking down at the dark street. He had to watch all the time. Watch this Millie and her dog now on top of all the rest of it. Keep himself and Orm safe from human treachery.

Standing at Millie's window, lonely, Aelf suddenly felt close to Orm, thought of him out there somewhere, a dragon in Oshkosh, hearing the same night sounds, smelling the same cool breeze as Aelf. "Orm, I am here," he whispered to the night wind, to no one.

THREE

A CLOSE ENCOUNTER

Henry Berg reached groggily for his alarm, shutting it off before his mother could hear it. For a minute he lay still, too close to sleep to remember why he had set it to go off an hour early, at 6:00. He sat up and shook himself. Vincent. That was it. Hiding Vincent before his mother made him get rid of him. Henry swung his feet to the floor and looked around for his pants. When he was dressed, he wrapped the terrarium in a torn blanket and, carrying it, crept quietly out of the apartment.

A couple of blocks over, by the river, Henry came to the vacant lot he'd thought of as the place to hide the lizard—in a grove of trees ten feet or so from shore. He climbed awkwardly across a low, makeshift wall of building rubble—chunks of concrete, broken-up bricks, hunks of wood with bent nails hanging out—dumped along the shoreline to stop erosion. His sweater caught on the NO TRESPASSING sign and Henry reached around to pull it off. All the junk dumped at the edge of the water was dangerous, especially for little kids. People, as far as Henry knew, did pretty much stay away.

Henry put the terrarium down. Stooping low, he walked along the pile of junk, looking for a good place. Not far from where he started, in a pile of cinderblocks and broken concrete, he found a small cave. Vincent's terrarium just fit. Standing a few feet back, Henry couldn't see Vincent at all. Perfect, he thought, smiling to himself. Vincent should be safe for the time being. Late May nights got down into the forties sometimes, but it wasn't likely to freeze. About the worst that could happen from cool weather was that Vincent would go into temporary hibernation. With two days' worth of mealworms and water sprinkled on the leaves in the terrarium, the lizard should be okay.

A couple of times, walking home, Henry turned and looked back. The sun reflected off the river and shifted through the leaves shaking in the wind. A pretty place. Quiet. In his kitchen, eating a bowl of cereal, Henry felt relaxed. Now Vincent was really his private discovery—nobody else even suspected where he was. Henry watched his mother pouring the orange juice, looking at him and chewing on her lip, getting ready to say something more about Mrs. Curtis. But she just handed him the juice and turned back to shut the refrigerator.

"Do you have all your work done, Henry?" she said. "All your homework?"

"Sure, Mom," Henry said. "I did it last night. While you were at the meeting."

She narrowed her eyes for a second, watching him, then sighed and went off to get dressed for work. "You could be doing so well, Henry," she said. "Everybody says that."

Sure they do, Henry thought to himself, everybody. Everybody thought he was an idiot. Some kind of jerk. A freak like his father. Actually, until Vincent hatched, that was pretty much what Henry thought himself. Now, knowing what he did about the lizard, being the only person who did know, Henry was starting to feel he might be somebody who could accomplish something. Henry Berg. The discoverer of one of the world's most mysterious animals, whether people knew it or not. Henry smiled to himself, carrying his cereal bowl to the sink.

Sitting in social studies class later on that morning Henry still felt good, even if he did get that icy cold feeling for a minute when Mrs. Curtis passed out the worksheet and he hadn't learned the stuff that went in the blanks. He sat there at his desk and thought about how, when the research he was doing at the public library was over, and he had figured out just what sort of animal Vincent was, everybody was going to be amazed. He was reading up on rare lizard species. Once he'd found the information he needed, and once Vincent had developed adult characteristics, then Henry could step forward and have everybody gasping.

"Pass up your papers, class." Henry jumped. He had been way off—nowhere near social studies class. There wasn't anything *on* his paper except his name. He passed it up. Michele, in front of him, looked at it and giggled. Henry just shrugged. So what? What people thought of him today didn't count. Let them laugh. Just wait.

"Good, Henry, that's a step in the right direction," his mother said that afternoon after school when he told her he'd given Vincent away. "I'm sure Tom will take good care of him."

"I'll go over to the library and do some work before supper, okay?"

"All right, fine." His mother smiled at him, with a look that said she was winning, a look that made Henry want to throw something at her, but instead he left, got on his bike, and rode off. When all this came out, she wouldn't be so sure she was always right about everything.

Coming into the reference room, Henry knew just where to go. A week ago he had found the perfect book—an enormous, technical guide to lizards and snakes with color photographs and descriptions of virtually every known type. Reading straight through it, eventually he ought to find Vincent. He pulled it down off the shelf, carried it to a table, and sat down, opening it to the D's, where he had left off.

That morning, waking up, Millie at first believed it was all nonsense. "Dreaming about dragons!" She laughed at herself. "Should have known better than to eat that can of sauerkraut in this warm weather." But when she opened the bathroom door, she shut it again in a hurry and stood leaning against the doorframe for a minute. Looking for something like his stone ledge in the cave, Aelf had finally gone to sleep in Millie's bathtub, his feet and tail hanging over to the floor. The whole tub was full of dragon, full of green skin pulsing up and down, up and down, as Aelf breathed deep in sleep.

For a second Millie almost rushed out, looking for people to come and see. Mr. Bickerstaff in the shoe repair place downstairs, that art student on the third floor, even the old drunk across the hall. Get everybody in to stare, to be amazed, to keep her company—not to leave her all alone with this dragon and the fear that rose up in her at the thought of the strangeness of it all. Last night it had all happened so fast, bang, bang, bang; one thing led to another, and Millie hadn't thought. Now, her bathtub full of lizard, her mind awhirl with wild stories about treasures and dragon eggs, in the ordinary sunlight of morning, Millie felt weak. But, no, nobody else could know about it. Because what would happen? Noise, confusion, TV cameras. Lights shining in everybody's faces. Aelf hadn't asked for that; Aelf had a real problem—he was trying to take care of his own young. Common decency demanded that she help him, that's all.

And keep herself out of it. "Out of it, Millie Levenson," she said to herself. A long habit, ordering herself sternly around, but necessary. She'd never been an easy person to keep in line, Millie thought, and sighed. But she was not going to use this dragon to make herself a celebrity. He was going to have a bad time of it anyway; there was no chance, Millie thought, that this egg could have sat around for almost a hundred years and hatched out. For one thing, something like that would have been on the news—network news even—and she watched Walter Cronkite almost every night. How on earth could an egg like that have survived? Somebody would have dropped it, lost it, fried it, made dragon meringue pie out of it; Millie knew she was getting silly, but the whole thing was so impossible even to imagine. The thing to do, she said to herself, was to go about the day in an ordinary way. To look at the situation step by step, the way she had last night. First, fix breakfast.

But even that had caused problems. Just as she sat down to a plate of fried egg and toast, it hit her. Eggs. Orm. My word, how would Aelf take it? And, just at that moment, he came in.

"Don't change anything because of me," Aelf said. But he sat off in the living room end of the apartment and made a cloud of smoke around himself. Probably the egg did bother him some; then she offered him something and found he wanted to gulp down a whole pound of hamburger she had in the refrigerator—raw. Best to get this show on the road, get this Orm found or prove it was impossible. Neither her pocketbook nor her stomach could stand having Aelf around for long. And Jack was still spending all his time under the table, peering out and growling every now and then.

"I'll check out that address on Washington Avenue, Aelf," Millie said, carrying her dishes to the sink. "You best stay inside as much as possible. Even with that raincoat and all, people would notice you."

Aelf stood unhappily in a corner of the living room, his head almost hidden by the smoke he puffed while he tried to think. "Jack will stay with me, then," he said, finally. "I will care for the dog, while you seek Orm."

Millie stopped washing the plate and stood, water running over her hand and down the drain. A kind of hostage. That's what that dragon was making out of Jack. In case she did something he didn't like. What had she gotten herself into? And her poor dog. She looked around at Jack, sitting under the table, rolling his eyes up at her.

"You won't hurt him?" she said anxiously. "Eat him, or anything?"

"He will be as safe with me as Orm would be with you, I assure you, Millie," Aelf said in his ponderous, slow-moving voice. Just in case she missed the point, Millie thought, he was spelling it out for her. Well, the thing to do was to get moving as fast as possible. She had let herself and Jack in for this; there was no way to go back.

"It won't take me long," she said on her way out the door, more to reassure Jack than Aelf. That dog looked stricken when he saw her heading out the door without him. If they got through this, she'd get the poor thing a sirloin steak.

Washington Avenue was only four blocks away. Millie planned to check out the address and see who was there. If Orm was there, Aelf could go in the middle of the night and get him back. The stealing part she was leaving up to him. Detective work was as far as Millie intended to take this thing. As she had feared, though, the address was a dead end.

The old house was four apartments now, all rented by people new in town. Millie talked to a young mother who lived downstairs. A real estate man owned the house. The young woman didn't know who the original owner had been. Millie went home for lunch, discouraged.

Walking home, though, she had another idea. Millie remembered Ruby Watson. That red-haired lady over at the high-rise who was a Daughter of the American Revolution and used to spend hours in the library, tracking down her ancestors. Ruby would spend half her time cranking the reading machine, looking at old newspapers on microfilm, chasing after dead Watsons like some old crow. Used to give Millie the creeps. But, come to think of it, those old newspapers could be just the thing now.

"Something as unusual as that, seeing those dragons, then coming back to town with the pouch and the egg, a story like that would have to end up in the newspaper," Millie told Aelf as soon as she came in. "And the newspaper would give names. Then we'd have something to go on."

"Can you do that today, too, Millie?" Aelf asked. The house being different, the people having moved on, all this made Aelf dizzy. Even the Old One had never thought of this. Going into libraries, poring over books, this was something no dragon could do. Reading the map was hard enough for Aelf—newspapers were past anything dragons would bother their brains over. "You can take Jack, too," he said suddenly, wanting her to know he respected her honor. Without her, Aelf could do nothing. For this part of it, he had to trust her. Better she see he trusted her, Aelf thought.

"Why sure, Aelf," Millie said warmly. "Just let me get a bite of lunch and take Jack for a little walk. I'll leave him here with you when I go to the library. They don't take kindly to dogs in the library." She smiled at him. "I know he's safe with you." Let him see it was a two-way street, Millie thought. He trusted her, she trusted him.

It was after 4:00 when Millie started for the library. Anyhow, she didn't have to fix supper for Aelf. He ate only every few days, he told her, and planned to go out at night and find his food. She hated to think what that probably meant—rabbits, rats, whatever small animals he could find, most likely. She just hoped nobody lost a cat.

Pushing through the turnstile into the reading room, Millie gave a start. That dark-haired boy near the information desk was studying pictures of lizards. It made her scalp prickle for a second, coming in and seeing that boy staring at drawings of reptiles when she was here herself to help out a dragon.

"Get a grip on yourself, Millie Levenson," she muttered under her breath. Boys were always interested in snakes and dinosaurs. What on earth could that have to do with Aelf? If she was this jumpy already, how much use was she going to be? Millie took two deep breaths and looked away from Henry, at the map of Oshkosh on the wall behind the desk, while she waited for the librarian to be free.

Poring over his book, Henry didn't notice Millie at first. He half-heard the librarian say, "1883?" and looked up, startled.

"Yes, the film for the second half of that year—the *Oshkosh Daily Wisconsinite*," Millie was saying.

Henry stared. 1883. The year of the "Enormous Egg, Marvel or Hoax?" story; the year Vincent's egg showed up in Oshkosh. What was going on? Then he shook himself.

"You've lost your mind, Berg," he whispered under his breath, and went back to his book. What could an old lady in a saggy purple sweater have to do with Vincent? There was a name for thinking that way—he'd read about it once—the situation where you get something on your mind and everything seems to connect to it. It was called some kind of phenomenon.

Henry started to read again. Not all that much was known about some types of lizards, he realized when he started to look closely at the book. There were gaps in the statistics for lots of them. Henry had an idea that at first had seemed fantastic, but now seemed more and more possible, as he eliminated type after type from the book. Maybe Vincent was some sort of dinosaur. Maybe his breed had survived in some isolated place up north.

"And here's my tyrannosaurus," he imagined himself saying casually to some kid who'd come over after school. "He's tame, but you have to be a little careful."

Across from Henry, Millie sat at the microfilm reader and cranked and stopped, cranked and stopped. The summer months were the ones she needed to check; the reel started in June. Millie worked it around to July, when Aelf said the men had carried off Orm. Once she got used to the blurry way the screen worked, Millie got really interested in the old papers. The ads for ladies' clothes and old medicines and the funny old headlines, such as "An Unrivaled Social Event" above an account of somebody's party, made it almost seem as if she'd moved back in time, as if she could walk back out and see wooden sidewalks and people in tall hats and long skirts. But that wasn't solving Aelf's problem, wasn't finding Orm. She began reading over the headlines on every page, starting in late June in case Aelf was a little off in his dates. Who knew if dragons and men used exactly the same calendar?

"Aggghhh!" Millie let out a loud gasp as if she were just amazed at something. The librarian came rushing over to the microfilm reader, looking worried.

"Mildred, are you all right?"

"I'm sorry, Jenny. Sorry to cause a disturbance. Just started to sneeze, that's all. You know, when you have to sneeze and you try not to?"

Henry looked at her, wondering; that was not a sneeze.

"Now you are here, though, Jenny, maybe you could help me out," Millie said. "You see this story here? Where it says 'Enormous Egg'? I want to copy that if I can. Ruby Watson told me you had some way to copy off stories she wanted, some other machine for that."

"Certainly. We'll just take this reel over to the other

reader and I'll show you how it works." The librarian took the microfilm off the machine and bustled off, with Millie following.

Now Henry was ready to let out some weird noise. He sat there, numb. Somebody after Vincent. How could that be? Who could know? Think. After his mother and Dr. Ferguson had refused to believe him, Henry hadn't talked to anybody about Vincent. What could be going on?

Henry got up and moved to a table on the other side of the library, so he could watch Millie. Once she and the librarian got her photocopy of the egg story, she stuffed it into her worn-out-looking brown plastic purse and pulled her sweater back on. She was leaving. Henry got up, too. Careful not to be too obvious, he followed along behind as she left the building.

He stayed a half-block behind her, ducking into a parking lot once and the doorway to an insurance building once to keep her from noticing he was following. She walked only three or four blocks, to that old building where the shoe repairman worked. She went in a different door, and Henry saw steps going up. There must be a broken-down apartment up there, he thought. He stood across the street for five or ten minutes, watching from a parking lot. But there wasn't anything to see. Nobody came out except a man carrying some shoes. Henry was worried, but he had to go home and eat dinner; he couldn't afford to stir up his mother again. It was time to get back home and think anyway; time to make plans.

─────────── FOUR ───────────
DRAGON SCENT

By the next morning—Saturday—Millie felt she and Aelf were getting somewhere. Once she had gotten hold of the Adolphous Berg name, Millie called Ruby Watson. People who looked around into their own families, listing out their ancestors, usually knew about other people's, too, especially important families like the Bergs.

"Millie, how are you, honey?" Ruby's family came from the South, and she still sounded like North Carolina.

"Ruby, I wonder if you can help me out," Millie said. "I'd like to find out something about an old Oshkosh family—the Bergs—Adolphous P. Berg, the old one was. Do you know what's become of the family? If any of them are still alive?"

"That's an interesting case, Millie. Very sad. Just shows what times are coming to, that family."

"What are you talking about, Ruby?" Millie said. Like many people who were big on ancestors, Ruby sometimes got carried away with how much better everything used to be. To listen to Ruby, you would think nobody ever murdered anybody, stole anything, or even used strong language up until twenty-five years ago.

"I don't think you'll find they're Jewish, Millie. Lutherans, I believe. If you're trying to connect a line of your family there, I'm afraid you'll find that's not a Jewish Berg line."

"No, that wasn't what I was thinking, Ruby. But what do you mean, 'sad'? Aren't there any more of them?"

"There are and there aren't, Millie." Ruby sighed. "I declare, it does make you feel bad. There's the son—spends summers at his place on Lake Winnebago, south of town. Most of the year he's in Arizona. Old Henry that is, and he has a grandson named for him, lives in town with his mother. The old man's son, John, turned out to be one of those protesters. Came back from the Vietnam War and never acted right after that. They even said he was a drug addict. Died off in a commune somewhere. His wife came back here with the little boy after that."

"Thanks, Ruby, that's a big help. I was trying to track them down for a friend who used to know one of them, years ago. Must have been the old Henry, I suppose."

"Glad to oblige, Millie," Ruby said. "You know I'm a walking history book." She laughed.

"I'll drop around for lunch at the high-rise sometime," Millie said. It felt good to be talking to somebody—Ruby was a little simple, but she was a kindhearted soul. Meant most of that about feeling so bad about people's troubles. "I've got something I can't get away from for a week or so," Millie said, "but after that I'll call you."

After she hung up, Millie checked the phone book. Four Bergs listed; one was the Henry that Ruby had mentioned, an address outside of town on the lake. Two others were men's names, and there was one A. That would be the daughter-in-law. An apartment over by the river, about six blocks from Millie's place. That would be the first place to check for Orm. The old man probably would not be back; usually it was into June before the summer people started coming in.

Millie looked around for a map to mark for Aelf. She found a felt-tipped pen and drew a red line from her apartment to the old man's house out Fond du Lac Road by the lake. Then she used green to trace a path over the five or six blocks to the river, to Henry's apartment house. She wanted it to be very clear and easy to read. Aelf wouldn't want to admit having trouble understanding the map.

After she got it worked out, Millie went into the bathroom to show the map to Aelf. He usually slept days, he'd told her, and had spent several hours both days lying in the tub, coiled and asleep. "Look at this, Aelf," Millie said, sitting down on the toilet lid and holding the map out for him to see. "There are two Bergs from that family in town now. See? The green line and the red one? The old man out by the lake, and his daughter-in-law here in town—lives with her little boy, Henry."

Aelf raised his head and extended a claw to take the map. He peered at it, holding it first very close to his snout, then backing it off more, holding it up in the air. His tail, hanging over the rim of the tub, twitched rhythmically, one, two, three; one, two, three, while he puzzled out the map. Millie just sat quietly and waited.

"Thank you, Millie," Aelf said, finally. "It is not easy, but I see where to go. Tonight I will begin the search for Orm."

"Don't get too upset if you don't find Orm now. It's possible the old man might have taken the egg to Arizona with him. You even have to consider, Aelf, that it's gotten lost, broken, destroyed somehow after all these years."

"Orm is here," Aelf said. "I will find him."

Aelf needed to stretch himself, to feel the dark and the night air. He didn't believe Millie's warnings about how something might have happened to Orm. Ninety-five years was not a long time. The treasures in the dragon cave were from the times when men came to Wales to build castles, before that, even, when men crouched behind the earth walls that curved around the hills like the folds of great dragons and hurled spears at one another. That was a long time, Aelf thought, the time when Hrothan was young— when there were shining swords to find, and helmets with the wings of birds carved at the sides. But Orm's life—just the time of an egg—that was hardly time at all. Maybe Millie knew something more than she was telling him. So busy all the time, rushing and bouncing around. She might be thinking anything.

Aelf settled back into the cool tub, wishing it were the

stone of his cave, wishing Grettir had never felt those warm winds across his skin. He shut his eyes and felt he was back, lying on the ledge with the others, staring at the piles of treasure that glittered when someone's eyes flashed, feeling at home.

Millie bustled about in the kitchen, feeding Jack, who had started to come out from under the table now, but who was not acting like himself. Having that dragon around took the starch right out of him; Millie was getting worried. "You're still in charge around here, Jack," she said. "He's just company after all. Wag your tail and bark all you want to. You live here." But Jack sat over by his dish and watched her getting his food out. Flattened right out, he was.

Millie poured out his food and scratched him behind the ears. Then she went in, put her feet up, and turned on the TV. Usually she waited for the news before she watched anything on TV. Today, waiting for dark and for Aelf to flap out her window, she would even watch a game show to get her mind off things.

After dinner, Millie went and stood at the bathroom door. She had to try one more time to get through to Aelf, to persuade him not to hurt anybody. "You will be careful?" she said, looking at all the green scaly loops of him coiled there in the tub. "You won't hurt anybody?"

Aelf sat up. "I was chosen to bring back Orm," he said stiffly. "That is what I must do." He looked up at her, standing in the doorway, twisting her hands together and frowning down at him. Suddenly he felt sorry, seeing Millie so upset. Without her, he would not have been going to look for

Orm; without her, he would never have found the places.

Aelf sighed. Owing a debt to humans, tangling the affairs of dragons and men together, made the whole difficult mission even harder. Now he had to worry about men as well as about Orm. Now, knowing Millie, he had a debt to her kind; feeling gratitude to her, he was no longer completely apart from men.

"I will be careful, Millie," he said, sighing again. "I will try not to hurt any human."

Seeing Aelf lying there, sighing and rubbing his snout, Millie felt suddenly worried about him as well. Really, he was in great danger himself and here she'd been worrying about the Bergs and not thinking enough about him. "You take care of yourself, too, Aelf," she said. "It's not just the people I'm worried about. It's you, too." She turned away and went back to the TV, leaving him to make his plans.

At 11:30 that night, Aelf pulled open the screen in Millie's back room, squeezed out, and flew over the empty parking lot. The air felt cool and whistled past him as he circled higher, getting as far up, as far away from the swishing cars and yapping dogs and droning TV sets as he could. Way up in the sky, Aelf stretched his wings and felt free again. Down below was the curve of the lake. He had to follow it out of town, to the old Henry's house where no one was living. Aelf planned to go there first, to give the young Henry and his mother time to be asleep if he had to follow Millie's map to their place too. Orm was going to be with one or the other, Aelf was sure. Where else could he be?

Once he was away from the streetlights and the bustle of the town, Aelf flew low, circled empty fields when he came to them, watching, ready to dive. Just the slightest sign, the tiniest flash of white bobbing across the grass, meant a rabbit out to find an early lettuce crop. Swoop, dip, grab. There was a flurry of kicking, some stray bits of fur in the air—and Aelf looking pleased. He ate three rabbits that way before he felt satisfied. By then it was after midnight.

Coming up along the shore, Aelf liked the sound of the water slapping, the smell of wet rock and slimy grass. Millie's map was easy to follow and he found the house with no trouble. It was dark and empty, set back on a lawn full of oak trees. Aelf settled onto the roof of the porch that ran across the front of the house, facing the lake. He padded gracefully across the shingles and squatted beside a window, examining it. Millie had shown him her storm windows and how they worked. He stuck his claws into the little slots where the catch was, and pulled the outside window out and laid it on the roof. Then he pushed up the inside window and squeezed in. He was in a bedroom.

Sheets were draped over all the furniture and shone in the light from his eyes—pale, moon-white, like ghosts. Aelf went slowly, shining his eyes like beacons into every room, sniffing under beds and behind bookcases, searching carefully for any sign of Orm or of the egg. Closet doors creaked when he pulled them open; plastic garment bags swished as he pushed them aside to shine his eyes behind them. Downstairs he startled himself by clanking up against the piano keys, shattering the quiet with a sudden burst of noise.

He went through every room in the house, peering inside the oven, even lying on the floor to see behind the furnace.

Hilde and Grettir being what they were, scatterbrained, he couldn't even be certain Orm had hatched. Their idea of the time might be off by a few months. So he could be looking for an egg or he could be looking for a dragon. He had to check inside drawers and cupboards, pull boxes out from under beds and suitcases down from shelves. He had to smell the air in every hall and every closet, hoping for some whiff of Orm. By the time he had searched every room, Aelf knew it was getting very late. He almost decided to go back to Millie's, to try young Henry's another night, but he couldn't face giving up. He couldn't face more days in her bathtub, not knowing where Orm might be. Aelf let himself back out the window again, turned, and pushed it shut. Then he flew back along the shore, following the line of the lake to Henry's apartment building.

There was a fishing dock just a half-block from Henry's building. Millie had marked it on the map and told Aelf to use it to know when he was in the right place. He lit there for a minute, looked around, saw the apartment building down the way, and spotted the upstairs window Millie had said would be Henry's.

As soon as he raised the screen and let himself in, Aelf's eyes glowed with excitement. He smelled Orm. He was sure—the faint musky smell of the smoky dark—too faint for any human nose, but he was sure. Orm. Aelf circled the living room carefully, sniffing the air, trying to follow the scent. Hah. He caught it, definitely stronger down the hall, toward the bedrooms. Aelf stopped outside the door to Henry's room. It was ajar, and he pushed it silently open.

He saw that the boy was sleeping, lying on his stomach, the pillow half over his head. Good, Aelf thought, it didn't look as if the boy would be easy to wake up. Very quietly, he moved around the room, looking, sniffing. He shone his eyes into the closet. Nothing. Then, beside the sleeping boy, where the smell was strongest, the pouch. The egg bag. Aelf held it in his claws and shook for a minute, shivering with relief—Orm was here, somewhere.

But he couldn't find where they had put him. The source of the smell was definitely the egg pouch. There was no other sign of Orm in the apartment. Aelf checked everywhere, his heart beating fast, shining his eyes under the sofa, inside kitchen cabinets, under the kitchen sink among the potatoes.

It was getting late, much later than he had intended to stay out. The sun was coming up; birds were cheeping. Aelf stood in the middle of Henry's living room, trying to think what to do. They must have hidden Orm somewhere else. The boy must have moved him. While he was standing there, thinking, a sudden buzzing started. Aelf jumped. Some human machine, making a noise he didn't understand. It was coming from the boy's room and it stopped as suddenly as it had started. Henry was moving around in there now; Aelf could hear him. Aelf wasn't sure what he was going to do about that boy.

All Millie's warnings came back to him. "You won't hurt anybody?" Aelf knew he could grab the boy, blow fire in his room, tear slits down his mattress, frighten him into saying where Orm was. That would be the dragon way. But knowing Millie, living in her apartment, made Aelf have doubts. Now he hesitated. Before he acted, Aelf would go back to Millie's tub to think. Perhaps he would even ask Millie what she thought.

Aelf had to get out fast; there was no time to squeeze through the window. He strode across the room, unlatched the living room door and rushed out, slamming it behind him in his haste.

FIVE

DRAGON BLOOD

When the alarm went off, Henry woke up right away. He had stayed away from the river and Vincent's cage ever since he'd seen the old lady in the library, just in case she was on to something, in case he was being watched. His plan was to get up at 4:30 Sunday morning and check on Vincent when nobody would be around. He reached over and pushed the buzzer on the clock back down. He swung his feet around and stood up. The door shut in the living room. He was sure. The front door. Somebody had just shut it.

Henry tiptoed through the kitchen and peered around through the dining area toward the living room and the front door. It was just barely light, but he couldn't see a sign of anything. He walked in. The TV set was there; the stereo. A burglar would have taken something. He tiptoed to his mother's room and listened. In the spring she had allergies and always snored. He heard her. Either it was his imagination, or whoever it was had been scared off by his alarm clock before he had a chance to take anything. Henry went back to his room and started to get dressed. Then he saw what was missing and his heart missed two beats. The pouch. Vincent's pouch had been on the table next to his bed. It was gone.

Trembling, Henry buttoned his shirt so fast he missed the top one and left the shirt hanging uneven at the bottom. If somebody was after the pouch, somebody was after Vincent. He had to get to the river fast and make sure Vincent was okay. Nobody was laying a finger on that lizard. Nobody. Running down the sidewalk, Henry felt more scared than he ever had before.

Vincent. That little lizard that scurried around and held its head to the side and looked up at him as if it thought he had some sense. That curled its tail around its nose and blinked at him when Henry sat on his bed and read in the afternoons. That trusted him. Henry had not thought it out before, but it was true. He knew it was. That lizard trusted him to protect it. It had hatched in his room. He was like its parents or something as far as Vincent was concerned. If something happened to Vincent, Henry would be to blame. He dashed across the street and ran across the lot, past the trees and to the piles of rubble.

The terrarium was still there, almost invisible under the broken concrete. Henry reached in and pulled it out. "Vincent!" The lizard came over to the corner closest to Henry's face and stood up; then something amazing happened. Vincent's eyes lit up. Like a lightning bug. When Henry said, "Vincent!" the lizard's eyes glimmered in a sudden flash of amber light. Henry leaned back against the pile of rubble and stared. He kept trying it and it kept working. "Vincent!" Flash. Over and over. He looked up and down the riverbank, back over behind him past the trees and across the lot to the street. Nobody. It wasn't five o'clock yet and it was Sunday morning. He took Vincent out of the terrarium and set him down on the ground.

Vincent went straight for the water. He scurried across the chunks of concrete and sat on the rocks, soaking his tail and his feet in the river and making his eyes glow, looking down to shine little beams of light into the water, chasing fish that way. Henry leaned back against the broken concrete and thought about being the owner of an animal like this one.

In that library book, he hadn't seen anything about a lizard that could light up his eyes. And if Vincent's eyes were doing this now, when he was just a few weeks old, what else might he do when he got older? Henry watched the lizard wading out a little in the river, dipping his nose in the water and looking back over at Henry as if he expected him to approve. Now that he thought about it, Henry remembered something about the psychology of animals that might have something to do with him and Vincent. He had read that a duck will automatically go up to whatever it sees when it hatches and mistake whatever it sees for its mother. Even if it was a dog or something. Imprinting, it was called. And the first thing Vincent had seen was him. So that meant Vincent would pattern himself after Henry. Look at Henry to figure things out. Follow him around.

Henry leaned back against the concrete chunks and thought how his life was going to change. From being a person that everybody looked down on, thought was weird, he was going to be a person everybody would want to know. All he had to do was to lie low, take good care of Vincent, and keep him a secret, while more and more of the unusual things about him started to show. He could take a lizard like this and be famous. Rich. People would pay to see them; people would chase along wanting his autograph. He could teach Vincent tricks, work up an act. It was obvious already that Vincent was very smart. Traveling around, doing guest appearances, they'd flatten everybody. Be rich and free as birds, he and Vincent. Go to Europe even. Henry leaned back and let himself imagine how it could be. Out from under being ordered around and not listened to. Out from under knowing people were wondering about his father, thinking about how he killed himself.

While he was planning it all, Henry let Vincent go farther than he meant to. Slussh, slussh, the gentle sound of something walking, wading in shallow water brought him back. Henry sat up and started after him, mad at himself. He couldn't be careless even for a minute; that old lady and whoever she was working with would be swooping down on his lizard, and he wouldn't have a prayer. Vincent had walked around a little bend in the shore; he was about twenty-five feet away. Henry started climbing over the pile of stuff between himself and the curve where Vincent was wading, when he saw something that made him freeze.

A cat was crouched, ready to spring. Just opposite Vincent. Flattened down the way they get—the end of its tail hanging over a lump of concrete, twitching, twitching, its body, still and crouched, in the instant before it was going to leap. It was a big cat, full of muscles that showed under its fur. Henry yelled, "Get out!" and ran as fast as he could. But it was too late. The cat leaped and Henry tripped, sprawling on the ground still fifteen feet away from Vincent. There was a furious splashing as the cat landed on the lizard.

Henry couldn't look. For a second he just shut his eyes. The splashing stopped. Not a sound. He looked again. The cat had fallen over and was lying, a dark blob at the edge of the water. Vincent was sitting beside it, his eyes glowing.

Henry rushed over. When he picked up Vincent, a horrible burning pain shot through his fingers. Gasping, he put the lizard down. The cat had torn a place on Vincent's back, and Vincent's blood, running down Henry's finger, had peeled away a strip of Henry's skin. It hurt terribly. Henry looked down at the cat. It was dead. Its legs jutted out like sticks from its body; its lips were rolled back from its teeth in an awful grin. The cat must have died in an instant, the second its teeth sank into Vincent's body. Henry shuddered. Vincent's blood was poison—a really deadly poison.

Henry backed off from the cat and the lizard, looking at

both of them. Vincent came up to him, holding his head cocked to the side the way he did, expecting Henry to do something. Probably his back hurt. Henry took off his shirt and wrapped the lizard in it. Carefully, he carried him over and put him back in the terrarium. Then he sat down for a moment, too stunned to move.

So there was even more to this lizard. Power. Death. A deadly weapon, really. No wonder people were after him. Henry looked over at the cat, a big striped tiger cat. Dead. He had to get out of here fast, before anyone came around. He was the owner of a powerful, deadly animal with strange glowing eyes. If he had wanted to be careful, to be secret before, now he had to be. He looked over at the terrarium. Vincent was lying down. That cut was probably bothering him some. Henry stood up; he would have to take care of him and see about the cut, clean it out with cotton. Be sure that he got extra food so he didn't get weak.

Carrying the terrarium, Henry headed home. It was quiet and peaceful, not a soul around. It seemed like a different world; like a different year, but it was just 6:00 A.M. when he got back to his room. As soon as he wiped off Vincent's cut, being careful not to get any blood on himself again, he shoved the lizard's terrarium to the back of his closet and lay down on the bed. Vincent's cut was not deep; Henry wasn't too worried about it. His finger was hurting, though, so he got up and got some Vaseline from the bathroom. He had an hour and a half to lie down and think before his mother would be getting up to teach Sunday school. He could use the time. Enough had happened in the last hour or so. He lay back on his bed and rested, shut his eyes and tried not to see that cat by the water.

When Millie got up Sunday morning, Aelf was waiting, holding the pouch, eager to tell her what he had found. "The boy has Orm," he said, holding out the pouch for her to see. "Look what was beside his bed. Orm's pouch."

"Are you sure it was Orm you smelled? Maybe it was just the pouch." Millie was amazed that anything had been there. After all these years, for the Berg boy to have that pouch right there on his bedside table! It was hard to believe. And now Millie found herself in a difficult position. She had to try to protect the Berg boy, and she had to help Aelf get Orm back. Millie did not like to back away; she always took responsibility on herself. Now she was getting worried. What if Aelf harmed Henry? There was no way she could think of to get help. Where could she go? To the police? They would either think she was insane, or, if she proved Aelf was here, they'd kill him. Kill him for sure, trying to cage him.

"The smell was too strong," Aelf said. "It wasn't just an egg. It was a dragon smell."

"Will the boy know that Orm is not just a lizard? Will he be able to tell he's a dragon?"

"Not yet," Aelf said. "But soon. Soon Orm will blow fire. Whoever tries to hold him will be burned. A boy cannot hold a dragon." Aelf's eyes glowed in sudden fierce pride.

Millie pursed her lips. She had to find a way to appeal to Aelf's sense of fairness, to make him see he owed Henry something. "Imagine that boy taking such good care of that egg, right up until it hatched!" she exclaimed. "And most kids today are so careless with their things."

But her plan backfired. Aelf got more upset. "Careless! With treasures? With young?" He twitched his tail and unsheathed his claws. "I have to get Orm back at once!"

"We've got to protect both of them, Aelf," Millie said. "You said yourself the boy helped to hatch the egg. Give him credit."

Aelf sighed. "Millie," he said, "I will not hurt the boy. Unless there is no other way. You have my word." In a way, Millie was right, Aelf knew. The boy didn't steal the egg. It was not Henry's fault Orm was here in Oshkosh. But Aelf hadn't done anything wrong either. And he had all this bother and crawling around humans' houses and having to make plans and follow maps when what he wanted was the smoky dark of his cave and the shine of his treasure. Now he was supposed to worry about Henry too. It was not fair to give him such a twisted path to follow.

"We need to watch Henry, to find out where he keeps the lizard," Millie said.

"There are three tall fir trees behind Henry's house," Aelf said. "I am going to wait there and watch. Late tonight I am going there—to be in place when the sun comes up. I will lie along a branch near the top, behind the needles."

"I see," Millie said. "You'll know where he goes, what direction. And then, when it's dark again, you can go yourself and look for Orm. From up in a tree you should be able to see for blocks, wherever Henry goes." She looked over at Aelf. "That's a smart idea."

"Thank you, Millie," Aelf said, slowly, impressively. He was proud that he had made his own plans, pleased he'd done it without any more help. It was his mission; the Old One had asked him. "And now," he said, "I am going to rest for the trip tonight. Excuse me." Aelf got off the sofa and strode back into the bathroom, to curl up one last time in Millie's tub and sleep until it got dark again.

Millie hitched the leash on Jack and went down the stairs to walk him around the block. She headed toward the vacant lot, where they usually went, the place they had met Aelf. But Jack wouldn't go. He tugged and pulled, sat right down on the sidewalk and skidded on his bottom to keep from going in that direction. Millie laughed and turned the other way, toward the river.

"You figure one dragon is enough, eh, Jack?" she chuckled. "Well, I must say, you have a point."

SIX

THE "ODD INCIDENT"

The next morning before dawn, Aelf settled himself in the middle fir tree in back of Henry's apartment building. There was a parking area, a narrow strip of grass, and then the three fir trees up next to the fence. The trees were taller than the building—Aelf could see the river a block away when the sun came up over it, rippling pink and blue and gold like the sky. There was a strong breeze up there and he dug his claws into the bark to steady himself. He had always liked the smell of pine needles in the sun.

In Millie's apartment he was always straining, always trying to make his mind go down the path where hers was. He had to watch his thoughts, and take care about what he said. Here, apart again, seeing man's world below him, he felt easy for the first time since he came. His scales soaked in the sun; he stretched out along a branch not far from the top, twining his tail around the trunk to give himself balance and support. His chin lay along the limb, his nose among the needles. Pine green with black wings folded, he wasn't easy to see. But why should anybody be looking up, staring into the tree for dragons?

In the morning when people started coming out of their houses, slamming car doors, roaring off with evil-smelling smoke coming from pipes under their cars, Aelf kept his eyes on Henry's door, waiting to see him get on a bicycle and go to school, as Millie had said he would. When Henry had gone off down the street, Aelf decided to doze. Millie had told him that it would be afternoon before the boy's school turned him loose, before he could be going to Orm.

Next door to Henry's apartment building lived old Harris Millet, who had been watching birds for five years, ever since he retired. Owned a pair of Sears Roebuck fifty-dollar binoculars that showed up every detail sharp as a pin. If they had been some cheap spyglasses like you get at one of those discount places, he said later, he would have figured it was some bump on the tree or something. But those Sears binoculars let you count the feathers on a robin's wing, read the print on the old newspaper they stuck in their nests. And now, he was seeing a monster. A lizard bigger than a man, or some kind of alligator—stretched out snoozing up in that fir tree. But with big black things like bat wings folded across his back. Harris Millet looked. He rubbed his eyes and wiped off his eyepieces and looked again. He followed the whole length of that monster, from its tail curled around the trunk to its nose resting on the needles way down at the end of the branch. He got up and went into the house.

In fifteen minutes he was back and a policeman was with him.

"I never saw anything like that!"

"Been lying there an hour or more!"

Voices down below. Aelf woke up with a start and looked down. Two men. Faces pointing up, staring at his tail and the hind part of his body wrapped around the trunk.

"There he is, my God, look at that monster!" The policeman pulled out his gun. "I'm not going up that tree, I'll tell you that!"

Aelf saw what was happening but he didn't blow fire. Even when he saw the gun, he held back. Millie's warnings, the Old One's cautions, echoed in his mind and made him hesitate. Aelf had been the guest of a human—he did not want to bring sorrow and death among them. Aelf stretched his wings to fly; Millet shouted, "I told you, it's some kind of flying alligator!" The policeman aimed his gun and fired. There was a sudden swirl of reddish smoke; a cloud of glowing pink haze surrounded the whole treetop and blinded them. Then nothing. When the smoke cleared there was no lizard, no monster, no Aelf. Nothing but a fir tree in the Monday morning sunlight in Oshkosh, Wisconsin.

"Damndest thing I ever saw," the policeman was saying. "Nobody's going to believe this." He stared up, blinking against the sun. "We'll get a ladder out here—check out the tree."

"We saw it; it had to be there." Millet kept pointing his binoculars up, searching for a sign that Aelf had been there. Even after the policeman filled in his report and got back in his car and drove off, old Harris Millet stood under the tree and watched and looked.

When Henry got back from school, he checked on Vincent in the closet first thing. He had kept him hidden so far, but he was going to have to think up something to tell his mother today. She would be snooping in the closet eventually. Very carefully, Henry unwrapped his shirt from around Vincent's body and looked at the cut. Already it was healing over. No need for a bandage anymore. The lizard was a little sluggish, though.

Henry sprinkled some fresh mealworms around for him and refilled his water bowl. Another day or so of resting in the dark would probably be all he needed to get back his strength. "Vincent!" he said, and watched his eyes glow. "Vincent! Vincent!" He could spend all day doing that. Amazing.

"Mom," Henry said at supper, "that lizard I gave Tom got sick. Acting sluggish and not eating right. I told Tom I'd keep him for a couple of days to see if I could get him back in shape. He hasn't had any experience raising lizards before."

"You brought that lizard back in here again, Henry?" His mother looked mean. "Without asking my permission?"

"I just got him today, Mom. I'm asking you now. I'm not

keeping him. Just treating him for a couple of days."

"If he didn't have my approval well, Henry, he doesn't have it sick. That's for sure. I don't see why that animal has to recuperate over here. If he's sick, take him back to the Pet Bazaar and get your money back."

"Just for two days, Mom. And Mr. Haase said if I could write up the research I do on him and on what might be wrong with him, I can get extra credit for science. I'm really trying to bring up my grades, like I promised."

"Today's Monday. Two days will make it Wednesday. Thursday morning I want to hear that lizard is back at Tom's or at the Pet Bazaar or somewhere, anywhere other than this house."

His mom really just didn't like lizards much more than she liked him, Henry thought. Both of them were weird, the way she saw it. Anyhow, he had gotten the time he needed—that was the important thing right now.

"Well, I guess I better get on with seeing about that lizard if he's going to be in shape by Wednesday," Henry said, getting up from the table. He went into his room and pulled out the terrarium. He wanted to look at Vincent and talk to him while he was lying on the bed. Just as he noticed some kind of new growths on Vincent's back, by his shoulders, his mother called.

"Henry! Come look at this!"

She was holding the afternoon paper, pointing out a story at the bottom of page two. "You aren't the only person with stories about remarkable lizards. Look what Mr. Millet next door saw today."

ODD INCIDENT REPORTED

Patrolman Harold R. Wacholz this morning fired into a tree at 1103 Riverview Avenue at what he and Harris T. Millet of 1105 Riverview said appeared to be an enormous alligator with wings. Millet, bird-watching in his yard next door, spied the protuberance in the tree and called the police. Wacholz confirmed Millet's opinion that there was a monster lizard coiled in the top of a fir tree at the back of the property. As he fired, Wacholz said, the creature attempted to fly away, spreading wings like a giant bat's. After the shot, a cloud of reddish smoke obscured their vision, both men say, and, when it cleared, there was no sign of a body, although Officer Wacholz was certain he hit the animal.

Both men remain convinced of their account of what happened, though a biologist at the university offered an alternate explanation. "A kind of parasite, related to the common puffball mushroom, sometimes reaches a rather large size and would release smoke or dust if hit," Dr. Hyatt Weber commented this afternoon. "Perceiving such an object as a monster lizard, once the suggestion was made, would not be impossible," Weber continued. "The human mind is almost infinitely suggestible and an unscientific observer is easily misled by unexpected sensory cues."

Henry read the story over twice. At first he was just surprised, couldn't believe there was another amazing lizard around. Then it hit him. He felt ice-cold. That was where his pouch went; that was what had stood beside his bed. The adult, looking for Vincent, come back for him. And now he was dead. The same red smoke around them when they die and when they are born, he thought. Henry was afraid; he had to get hold of himself, not let his mother see how it was hitting him. "That's wild," he said, trying to sound as if he didn't believe it.

"It's getting to be a regular disease." His mother laughed. "But, still, it's awfully strange, isn't it?" She looked at Henry hard. "It really gave me a start. I thought for a minute your lizard *had* hatched out of the egg in a cloud of smoke."

"Wow, Mom," Henry said, "old age is softening your brain. Pretty soon you'll be seeing things yourself." It worked. She laughed and relaxed.

"I guess old Mr. Millet just hasn't got enough to do over there all day," she said. "Especially since his wife died. We ought to have him over some evening for cake or something."

Henry went back to his room and sat. He looked at the beginnings of wings on Vincent's back. He shut his eyes. He saw that cat, dead and stiff. He saw the enormous bat-winged monster coiled in the tree; he saw him creeping by his bed, looking, watching for Vincent. By himself in his room, not needing to pretend, Henry started to tremble, as if he were cold.

Millie read the newspaper story over twice. At first she told herself he had flown off, that the smoke was just to conceal his flight, to help him get away. But she knew what must have happened. The old familiar rage and sorrow swept over her and she leaned her elbows on the table and cried. Why, why, why couldn't people live without this fear, this horror of everything different? Poor Aelf, not very bright compared to people, not here because he wanted to be, not trying to hurt anybody. Dead. And here was some moron expert explaining that he was really just a mushroom or something. A giant tree toadstool. Even though she was crying, Millie laughed at that. A bitter kind of strangled laugh that was halfway a cough. Why couldn't people have a little decent humility and let things live? Why couldn't they find out about something first instead of shooting it?

But anyway, she thought, sad as it was at least it was over. No more jumping at the sight of her bathtub in the morning. No more worrying about whose cat or dog he might be swallowing down. In a way it was nature, after all.

Now she was out of it. Millie carried her dinner dishes in and started washing them. Now she could call Ruby and plan that lunch she'd promised. Now she and Jack could get back to normal life. It was always a chancy business—Aelf had known that. And he might have killed somebody himself; he was ready to, Millie knew.

"Now it's over and you're out of it, Millie Levenson," she said to herself out loud, wiping the pan that was too big to fit in the dish drainer. "No more dragons and worry and nightmares and night walks for you." She walked in the living room and flipped on the TV. Before it even came into focus, she turned it off. She walked into the bathroom and found herself staring into the tub, seeing Aelf there. Millie shook herself.

"Fidgety as a cat!" she said. "Get a grip on yourself, girl." But Millie knew from past experience that when she got into this kind of state, walking around, talking to herself, unable to sit still, there was some thing she wasn't facing up to. Her conscience was after her somehow. Millie had a terrible conscience.

Now, saying to herself again and again that it was all over, Millie knew it wasn't. Down inside herself, a voice was telling her she had a responsibility in this. And she didn't want to hear it.

"Is it my business to save baby dragons?" she snapped at Jack, who was watching her pace around.

"Who else?" responded the voice inside her. No matter how she tried to back away from it, she knew she was the only one. Maybe they could send another dragon, but what luck could he possibly have? And suppose nobody did anything? Suppose Orm started to grow up in Oshkosh, becoming more and more obviously a dragon? Wouldn't people start hunting the rest of them, stir around those caves in Wales where Aelf's relatives had been for centuries? Wouldn't there be more killing and dying? And what about the boy—Henry? Didn't she have a responsibility to him, knowing what she did? How would Millie feel if she picked up the paper one day and read how a little boy had been set on fire by his pet lizard? Could she live with herself?

And then there was Aelf. Tears came back to her eyes and stung her nose when she thought of Aelf. Harping on him from the day he came about being careful. Never giving him a moment's peace about not hurting anybody. Maybe if she hadn't been after him all the time, he would have defended himself better, gotten away. Maybe it was partly her fault he'd been shot.

Millie heaved an enormous sigh and sat down. "All right. All right. If I can do it, I will," she said. She leaned back and wiped her face with the dish towel she suddenly discovered she'd been carrying around through all her pacing and rambling. "The next question is how? How can one creaky old lady rescue a dragon in distress?" Millie leaned back in her recliner and half-laughed and completely cried for another half-hour. Then she washed her face and went to bed.

SEVEN
SAY "THANK YOU," HENRY

On Tuesday night Henry was in his room, getting ready to move Vincent to a safe place Wednesday. Growing so fast he was already big for the terrarium, Vincent might well get loose unless Henry fixed a bigger, stronger cage for him. His plan now was to get Vincent out to his grandfather's place on the lake and hide him in the boathouse. For a few weeks, until his grandparents got back for the summer, it would be safe. Taxi fare out there was $3.50, which he had saved up; he and his mother had taken a taxi out there once before when the car was in the shop.

Practical things, like how much taxis cost, he always re-membered, Henry thought. He was still feeling jumpy from a test in school that day. He'd been feeling too worried about Vincent to think anyhow, and they had had one of those fill-in-the-blanks idiot quizzes on how long various islands off Australia were.

"It's insulting, Vincent," he said. "They just want to order you around. The dumber the stuff they order you to memorize the better. Then they can sit around drinking coffee and laughing over what fools they're making of you. 'That Berg kid thinks he's pretty hot stuff, but he'll knuckle under, wait and see.'" Henry laughed his favorite old crone laugh like the witch in the Snow White movie his grandmother had taken him to when he was little. "See this delicious apple, sweet little girl?" He got further into the witch act, using a cracked, weird voice, putting on a good show for Vincent, who, even more than he used to, was showing interest in talk. When Henry said anything, the lizard sat up and listened, his head cocked to the side, as if he were straining a little to hear everything. He also looked interested in watching Henry fix the cage. A lot of company Vincent was getting to be, more like a friend than an animal.

Dr. Ferguson was over having dessert and coffee with his mother. Henry could hear them talking, a drone of voices in the living room. He didn't pay much attention. Ferguson wouldn't mess around with him, being so interested in his mother and all. At least he was an improvement over that Green Bay Packer fan she went around with last fall who kept on dragging Henry out to throw a football with him and was always doing knee bends and saying "hup, hup, hup!"

What Henry dreaded with his mother's boyfriends was

when they started to get really interested in her and figured it was time to start buttering up the kid. He wasn't Henry to them, just "the boy"—Ann's weird kid. Ferguson, he had to admit, hadn't been bad so far. Hadn't been thumping around, slapping him on the back or rumpling his hair, wondering how school was or how the girls were, or anything revolting like that. But he was bound to be starting in sooner or later, if he kept seeing as much of his mother as it looked like he was going to.

Henry used the staple gun and fastened the wire around the front of the cage. "You're going to like this, Vincent," he said. "Lots of air this way. It's cooler than that terrarium and bigger."

"Making a cage, Henry?" Dr. Ferguson all of a sudden was standing in the doorway. Henry jumped; he hadn't heard him come up.

"Sorry if I startled you," he said. "Ann said you were turning into a real scientist with this lizard of yours. I thought I might take a look." He came into the room and looked down at Vincent.

"Yeah, well, really he's Tom's lizard now. I'm just trying to get him a better cage and stuff. See what's wrong with him. Tomorrow, Tom's getting him back."

"Your mother said you were just baby-sitting for him." Dr. Ferguson sort of chuckled. "Hasn't he grown quite a bit?" Dr. Ferguson leaned over and reached into the terrarium, to run his finger along Vincent's back. "And what are these growths starting to form here along his shoulders?" He pointed to the stubby beginnings of what Henry had figured must be wings along Vincent's back. Then he drew back, shaking his finger and blowing on it. "Ow!" Dr. Ferguson looked at the end of his finger in surprise.

Oh, good grief. Henry realized with a sinking feeling that Vincent's cut wasn't healed completely, that it was still leaking some. Not that he much cared if Dr. Ferguson got burned, poking around. But that was the sort of thing that was sure to set off his mother. Get her talking about Vincent's being dangerous, give her the perfect excuse to boot the lizard out the door right this minute.

Dr. Ferguson stood there frowning. Then he came over and looked at Henry's hands. He saw the red streak down his middle finger. "Happened to you too, I see," Ferguson said, acting worried. "Henry, some kinds of venom in reptiles can be very dangerous."

"It's okay," Henry said. "It's just that his blood burns your skin a little. He's really gentle and all. He isn't going to hurt anybody."

"I wouldn't be too sure," Ferguson said. "I know Ann is a little too nervous about animals like this. But this isn't anything to ignore either. You might get hurt."

"Naw," Henry said. "I'm careful. Until that cut heals, I'll use a rag if I have to pick him up. And no pet store is going to be selling poison lizards to kids. They could get sued or something."

"Well, maybe the wrong kind got mixed in with a shipment," Dr. Ferguson said. "He just doesn't look quite right to me, anyway, when I start to think about it. Hasn't he grown awfully fast? I'm no herpetologist, but I would think he's unusually big." He stooped down to eye-level with Vincent's terrarium. Vincent was scratching around with his back to him, digging for mealworms under his newspaper. "What did Ann say you'd named him?" Dr. Ferguson asked.

Henry went cold. That would be the end. He tried to think of something to say, to change the subject before it happened. But his brain stuck. Nothing came. And then Ferguson remembered.

"VINCENT!" he said at the top of his lungs, right in the lizard's ear.

BLAZE. Those eyes never flashed so bright, Henry thought bitterly, never.

"Look at that!" Dr. Ferguson took two steps back. "Did you see that, Henry?" He stood there looking astounded.

Henry felt weak. This was not the time. Everything was going to get wrecked. Henry was trying to think how to save the whole thing, but making his brain move was like trying to run through hip-deep mud. He was frozen, watching, waiting for Ferguson to say it again. For the whole situation to get completely hopeless.

"Vincent!" Dr. Ferguson said again. Blink. "Vincent!" Blink. Henry felt sick. "This phosphorescent reaction is remarkable, Henry!" Dr. Ferguson said.

"It's just some kind of chemical," Henry said. "Like lightning bugs, some jellyfish. Nothing very unusual about it."

"I think you're wrong there, Henry," Dr. Ferguson said. "The way the response is cued by the name. Must be something in the wavelengths, the pitch vibrations, that sets up the reaction." He stared down at Vincent, shaking his head. "This just doesn't seem to be any ordinary pet store lizard, Henry."

"What?" Henry's mother had come in. "What do you mean, Jim? What's unusual about it?" She came in and sat on the bed and Dr. Ferguson started telling her all the remarkable things about Vincent, starting with the fact that his blood seemed to be poisonous. Henry just stood there, helpless. When he had tried to tell them in the first place, were they interested in listening? Now that he didn't want them to know, didn't need them to butt in, here they were.

Henry's mother just sat there, looking more and more worried while Ferguson showed her Vincent's back, got his eyes to glow. Actually, once she'd learned that the blood burned the skin off a person's hand that was just it, Henry knew, for her. She'd always been picking away, afraid he'd break a bone if he climbed a tree, crash into a car on his bike, put out his eyes with sparklers on the Fourth of July when his grandfather managed to sneak him a couple. Now, as soon as she'd taken a good look at Henry's finger, rushed off for ointment and gauze and one thing and another, that was it.

"You can't keep that lizard in here, Henry," she said. "I don't want that creature in here even for one more night. For one more minute. You might as well have a pet rattlesnake."

"Henry has been careful, Ann," Dr. Ferguson said. "He's

done a good job and he doesn't seem to be taking unnecessary chances."

"I don't care, Jim," she said. "I can't take it—thinking something might happen. That thing might bite him."

"Mom, Vincent isn't going to bite me. He's never bitten anything." That was true, Henry thought. Nobody was asking what might happen if something bit Vincent. "I promised Tom, anyway. I've got to give him back tomorrow."

"Well, wait a minute here, let's think," Dr. Ferguson said. "I don't think you ought to do that, Henry—give this lizard to Tom to keep. Especially since you said yourself he's less experienced than you are."

"Exactly," his mother said. "You can't pass a monster like that around as if it were a hamster or something."

"You aren't going to try to kill him!" Henry was really getting scared now.

"Well, Henry," his mother said, "I don't see how we can have children playing with an animal that might turn out to be very dangerous. It should never have been taken out of the jungle where it belonged. I'd like to give that pet store man a piece of my mind!"

"Well, hold on a minute," Dr. Ferguson said. "I don't think it'll have to come to that. Look here, Henry. I think your mother is right. You could get hurt. And you don't have the facilities for keeping Vincent properly. He should be handled with special gloves and so on. But, listen, I do. Over at the lab at school. We do a lot of learning studies with rats and mice. Have cages and a controlled environment for keeping small animals. I could take him on over there, where nobody could get hurt. We could watch him, see what he develops into. I could have a guy I know in biology come and take a look at him. And there's no reason why you couldn't come over, too. See as much of him as you like."

"But he really belongs to Tom," Henry said. That was all he could think of to say, and he knew it wouldn't do any good. "I can't just give away Tom's lizard. After I just told him he could have it."

"You'll just have to explain what happened, Henry," his mother said. "We're trying to protect Tom and you. And it's really awfully nice of Jim to offer to do this for you boys. Don't forget that. You be sure and thank him."

"It's okay, Ann," Ferguson said. "I'm interested in him myself. I never saw anything like those eyes. Never."

So that was that. Henry had to sit there and watch Vincent going out the door. Sitting in his terrarium, looking back over his shoulder at Henry, his eyes just barely glowing, he was carried straight out the door by Mr. Nice Guy in person, good old Dr. Ferguson. And Henry had to act grateful on top of everything else. "Say 'Thank you,' Henry." That was just about the last straw. Saying thank you to the person who was taking the only thing he cared about away from him. To the one who was killing every chance he had to be somebody, to have people take notice.

Henry lay back on his bed, stiff with anger. Friday, he was supposed to go over to the lab and see Vincent. Friday, he was invited to look in at his own lizard. How long would anybody remember Vincent was his? Until he grew wings, like the one in the tree? Until he was seven feet tall? Forget it. Now he was Ferguson's lizard, Ferguson's discovery. And all Henry could do was put up with it. Act grateful, even.

Henry lay back on his bed and stared at the ceiling and took three deep breaths, calming himself down. He needed time to think, to back off from all this. To get into his trick of being someplace else, some *thing* else. But he didn't feel like sliding down into the river water, not tonight. Instead, he thought himself out into space, into the quiet and the dark, out there on the edge of the universe. Somehow Vincent's coming had made him wonder about what was out there. Then reading about the other lizard, the big winged one, had made him wonder even more. One kind of mystery made you think about all of them, made you see that the world wasn't that simple, Henry thought.

Henry lay on his bed and thought himself out to the edges of the Milky Way, out past almost everything. Then he tried to turn around and feel himself coming back, back into the solar system, to another planet. Now he was on the surface of Jupiter, heavy, heavy, weighing a ton, looking up through the reddish choking atmosphere at the twelve moons lighting the sky. Jupiter was out there, existing at this moment as much as he was. And so were the great winged lizards that Vincent had come from—somewhere, off in the woods, or deep in caves, far away from human beings.

Henry had to work on a plan, to figure out a way to get

Vincent back from the lab. People would have to face the fact that Vincent was his lizard. But tonight, after everything that had happened, he was too tired to plan. Tonight he just lay there on his bed and let himself float in the dark and the mystery of it all. Tomorrow he would get up and start making plans.

EIGHT
THE CLEANING LADY

Millie thought about how to approach Henry Berg. Not knowing what was happening on his side—not even whether the Bergs realized the lizard was a dragon—made it very difficult to plan. Finally she decided the only thing was to be direct. It was the boy who'd had the pouch; it was the boy she would go to. She would wait for him after school, simply watch for him riding back on his bike, walk up to him with the pouch Aelf had taken from his room and say, "I believe this belongs to you?"

"No!" was what Henry said on Wednesday afternoon, when all of a sudden there was the old lady from the library standing on the sidewalk, shoving Vincent's pouch under his nose. "I never saw it before!" he said, scared out of his wits.

"If you have a baby lizard that hatched from this pouch,

you should let me talk to you. You might get hurt. Really, I just want to help you," Millie said earnestly, watching as Henry turned pale. He was almost shaking. So he did have Orm.

"You must be crazy," Henry said, looking around wildly, wondering if a giant lizard was lurking behind her somewhere.

"Most people would say so," Millie said. "That's for sure. But I think you know I'm not. Listen. I never meant to get into this, any more than you did. You probably don't know what to think about any of it. You've got to let me explain what I know."

"Why?" Henry said. "I don't have any lizard. Maybe I used to have one. Maybe I used to have one until last night. But now I don't. So don't send any monsters creeping around in the middle of the night. Not at my house." Henry was mad as well as afraid. Everybody in the world was after him, pestering him.

"What happened?" Millie asked. "Where did you take it?"

"I didn't take it anywhere," Henry said. "I was taking good care of it. It's my lizard." He looked straight at her, waiting for her to reply, but she didn't. "It's my lizard, and I was building it a bigger cage. Somebody else took it. You want to sneak around, stealing people's lizards, tell your friend to head over to the university. That's where he is. In a lab over there."

"Oh, no!" Millie took two steps back and stared at Henry. "At the university! They'll be running experiments, writing it up—making that lizard into a freak show!" She looked at Henry in horror. "We can't let that happen!" The end of the dragons' private world in their caves. That would be the result of the university's studying Orm. The beginning of people prying and poking, cages and killing.

Henry was confused. He couldn't see what this lady wanted. She seemed to be doing what he had been trying to do—keeping Vincent secret. But why? And how many more giant lizards did she have lurking around somewhere?

"What about the big ones?" he asked, peering down the sidewalk. "How many of them are there?" There wasn't anybody in sight—just the paper boy a block away.

"They only sent Aelf," Millie said, "I swear to you, Henry, that was all. And look what happened to him."

"I don't see what you want me for," Henry said. "I can't see what your problem is."

"I saw you in the library," Millie said. "I didn't know who you were then, of course. But now I know why you were looking through that reptile book. You *know* there's something strange about that lizard. You know it, but you don't know what. Am I right?"

"In a way," Henry said.

"Well, I can tell you," Millie said. "You probably won't believe me at first, but I can tell you. As far as I can see, it's up to you and me now to do something. We have to stop it."

"Stop what?" Henry said. "Vincent is okay. They'll take care of him."

"Stop them studying that baby lizard before it starts to grow into what it is."

Henry pushed his bicycle back and forth while he talked, trying to think straight. "Well, what is it, then?" he said defiantly, looking up at Millie. "You keep saying you know all this. What do you know?" His heart beat faster. "What is it?"

Millie didn't know what to say. The paper boy was getting closer, just a few houses away, and he was looking at them with curiosity. They must look strange, standing there talking so seriously. She had to get Henry to come back to her apartment, to let her explain. She just had to trust him, that was all. There wasn't anything to do but tell him the truth.

"A dragon," Millie said. "I know it's unbelievable. But that's what it is. A dragon."

Henry just stood on the sidewalk and stared at her. A dragon! Come on! He'd thought about dinosaurs; he was ready to believe almost anything. But a dragon?

"What?" he said. That was all he could manage to do. Just stand there on the sidewalk and say, "what?" two or three times. Jason from school, delivering the paper, swerved around them and stared, obviously wondering what was going on.

"I know," Millie said, as soon as Jason was past. "I know how you feel. But you have to give me a chance. If you just go a step at a time, like I did, it doesn't seem so strange. Look, we have to get off the sidewalk and talk. Come on home with me for an hour or so. Let me show you where Aelf stayed. Explain what he said. Then you'll believe me."

Henry rubbed his head. He didn't know what to think.

This lady might be nuts, but he just about had to go along with her. Not being the only person to know about Vincent was in a way a relief. It was beginning to seem as if it might be too big a mystery, too complicated and full of dangers for one kid to cope with. Just to talk to somebody about it would be a help.

"All right," he said, and they walked off together down the sidewalk, to Millie's place.

Sitting in Millie's living room, hearing about the everyday details, how Aelf had slept in the bathtub and eaten raw hamburger, Henry began to see the whole thing. He started to calm down. But he wasn't sure of what to do. Millie expected him to see it her way. She wanted him to help keep the dragons' secret forever.

"They aren't really very smart, Henry," Millie said, leaning forward, her glasses sliding down her nose. "They're kind of pathetic, really, trying to think." She told him about Aelf struggling to figure out maps, about his wonderful plan to disguise himself in a raincoat. "But they do care about each other. Why else would Aelf have taken a chance like that?"

"But Vincent was born in Oshkosh," Henry said. "He's not really a Welsh dragon. Why couldn't we have dragons over here now?"

"Because they wouldn't fit in," Millie said. "Because people wouldn't let them be what they are. Look at what happened to Aelf."

"Well, if people knew what he was, maybe they wouldn't have shot him," Henry said. "Imagine what people would think, how excited they'd be if you gave them the chance to see a real dragon. Flying, talking, blowing fire and smoke." Millie had told him about all the things Aelf could do. It made his ideas for an act with Vincent seem even better. They could really be famous; people would look at him as if he were somebody, somebody important. Really, that was more sensible than Millie's plan just to stuff Vincent back in some dark cave in Wales.

"And besides, Henry," Millie said, sipping some of the Coke she had gotten for the two of them, "you can't forget they are dangerous. Vincent will want his cave. He will want to be with the others. You could even be killed, trying to keep him."

"Well," Henry said. "It seems to me he ought to decide. If he can talk and think and all. I don't see why we have to be so busy deciding what he ought to do with his life. He's like a citizen of Oshkosh now. Isn't it his business, too?" Henry remembered how Vincent had looked over at him Sunday morning when he was wading in the river. Like Henry was his father or something. Henry didn't want to just ship him off, dump him in some cave, and never see him again.

"I can see how you feel, Henry," Millie said. "And I'm not trying to tell you what to do. I haven't got any right to do that. Let's just go at this one step at a time. Both of us agree the first thing is to get him out of that lab over at the university. Unless we can do that, we might as well forget about the rest of it."

"Yeah," Henry said, "you're right." And he sighed. In the

excitement of hearing Millie's story, he'd almost forgotten that Vincent was gone. Remembering, he felt silly for getting so worked up over what to do. He'd never have the chance to decide. How could he and Millie get him out of that lab? The place was bound to be locked up at night, and all day there'd be people around.

"You're going over there on Friday?" Millie asked. "Well, listen. I think we can work out a plan."

It turned out Millie knew a lady down at the old people's high-rise, who used to be a cleaning lady at the university. She'd talked about it a lot. Millie's plan was to get herself one of those green coats like the cleaning ladies wore on the job, and pretend to work there. She could get into the lab that way.

"If you just walk right into a situation like that, act like you belong there," she said, "you've got a good chance. People hate to make fools of themselves. Even if they think something is strange, they usually won't ask about it."

Millie wanted to time the whole thing so that she and Henry would be in the lab at the same time, late Friday afternoon. Henry's job would be to get Dr. Ferguson out, to leave her alone with Vincent long enough for her to get him into a box, and out of the building. Then she could catch the bus and bring him back to her apartment.

"We'll just have to hope that nobody else will be around the lab," she said. "Friday afternoon is usually a pretty dead time around schools."

"Yeah," Henry said. "Dr. Ferguson said Friday was a

good time because I wouldn't get in anybody's way."

"So, we'll get him back here, and then decide what to do. Okay, Henry?"

"Okay, Millie," Henry said, getting up to go. "And, look, I'm sorry I was so jumpy when I saw you on the sidewalk before."

"Listen, Henry," Millie said, "you'd have to be crazy not to be jumpy after all this." She walked over to the door with him and came out to the landing. "See you Friday!" she called down.

"Friday, Millie!" he called back up.

When Henry and Dr. Ferguson walked into the lab, Henry felt cold and a little dizzy. Partly because he was worried about the plan he had made with Millie, partly because he was going to see Vincent, to look at him for the first time knowing what he was. He was only halfway listening to Dr. Ferguson.

"We've been varying the lighting in here, trying to get the best conditions for him," said Dr. Ferguson. "He is nocturnal, of course, as you said." They walked over to Vincent's wire cage. It had a door at the top; Henry could see it wasn't locked.

"Vincent!" he said. The little dragon turned around at once, his eyes glowing, and ran to the front of the cage to see Henry.

"Well, he looks glad to see you," Dr. Ferguson said. "Really, of course, he's a little out of our line." He pointed to the rows of wire cages lining the other side of the room. "Rats, we are set up for; lizards are more the business of the biology department. Say, Henry, I did get a herpetologist— that's a reptile man—over to look at him. And he was very interested. Shared my opinion that we're on to something unusual here." Dr. Ferguson smiled down at Henry. "He said he has a number of early characteristics. Shares some with the dinosaurs, in fact."

"Really?" Henry said.

"He feels he may grow to be quite large," Dr. Ferguson said. "Perhaps as big as a small dog."

"That big!" Henry said.

"Surprising, isn't it?" Dr. Ferguson said. "Makes you wonder where the Pet Bazaar man got him. I went down and talked to him, but he wasn't much help. Claimed he'd never sold a lizard like this one. Said he only sold iguanas from Mexico. Maybe this is a genetic throwback. Or some rare form that got mixed in with an iguana shipment." He looked up, startled, at a cleaning woman who came in the door, pushing a big broom along in front of her.

"Doesn't Louise usually clean in here later in the evening?" he asked.

"Illness in her family," the woman said. "She was called home sudden. I'm subbing for her."

"Well, all right," Dr. Ferguson said brusquely. "But be careful in here. We have a lot of expensive equipment. Don't move anything; don't touch any dials or adjust any of the machines in any way."

Making a big effort, Henry kept himself from looking at Millie. He turned to the other side of the room. "Show me these rats over here," Henry said. "What are you doing with them?"

"Studying the effect of overstimulation and overcrowding on their nervous systems," Dr. Ferguson said. "Look at this." They walked over. In one cage the rats were healthy looking, sleek and alert. Henry leaned over and looked at them. In the next cage the animals were bony and listless. They just lay there, not interested in anything. "There's no difference in the diet of these specimens," Dr. Ferguson said. "The ones on the left have been subjected to mild electric stimulation and to an overcrowded environment."

As he went on to explain in more detail, Henry started. "Electric stimulation! Are you shocking Vincent?" He looked over at the dragon, who was now asleep at the back of his cage. Millie moved to that side of the room, pushing her broom in front of her.

"We used a minimum of electric stimulus on him in one experiment," Dr. Ferguson said. "An animal of that sort doesn't have a large cerebral cortex, Henry. He's a cute little fellow, and he's certainly interesting, but you don't want to turn him into a human."

"I don't want anybody hurting him is all," Henry said.

"We wouldn't do anything to hurt him. Don't worry. He's being taken care of. Eats like a pig, the lab assistant says. Be glad you got him moved out, Henry. You'd go broke feeding him." Dr. Ferguson laughed.

"Could I see your office, too?" Henry said. "Where you write up your research and all?" Henry and Millie had been right. There was nobody in the lab but the three of them.

"Sure, Henry." Dr. Ferguson looked pleased. "I've got to pick up some things before I leave anyway. Why don't we just go down the hall a minute and collect my papers? By then the cleaning woman should be finished and I'll check out the lab and lock it up before we leave."

Henry managed to keep him talking for almost ten minutes in his office, by asking lots of questions. Dr. Ferguson, to Henry's relief, was the kind of guy who really liked to talk.

"Well, now, Henry," he said after Henry had asked all the questions he could think of, "let's just go down and say goodnight to that lizard. Then we can lock up and head for home, and see what your mother has cooked up for dinner." He patted Henry on the shoulder and they walked down to the lab. Millie was gone. So, Henry saw at once, was Vincent.

"What the devil!" exclaimed Dr. Ferguson when he saw the empty cage. "That fool cleaning woman must have let him out somehow. We've got to find him, Henry."

Crawling around on the floor, looking under boxes and behind cabinets, Henry watched the clock on the wall: 4:45. The time the bus came. He saw the long hand click past the 9 and he smiled to himself. There went Vincent, home to Millie's in the box. Just the way they'd planned it. Perfect.

It could hardly have been smoother. And Dr. Ferguson and his mother could never suspect he'd had anything to do with it. Vincent was safe. He and Millie had done it.

NINE

THE DECENT THING

With Vincent back at Millie's, Henry had to figure out what he really thought was the best thing to do. Sitting in Millie's living room, talking it out, he could tell she would never see it his way. "Decent," she kept saying. The "decent" thing to do was to take Orm back to the hills in Wales, so he could live where he belonged. And she was willing to spend her own money, money she had saved up for her funeral, to pay for a ticket to Wales. "Better to do one last decent thing," she said, "than just to go under the ground in style."

Henry kept thinking one way and then the other. For one thing, it didn't seem nice to use up Millie's money that way. Should he really let her do it? And, besides, why should he have to give up all his plans? Didn't Vincent really want to stay with him? Didn't he always run right up, eyes glowing, when Henry leaned over Millie's tub to look at him? Henry lay on Millie's floor and let Vincent run around on top of him, pulling on his shirt and sticking his nose down in his pockets, and he thought.

It was Monday afternoon, after school. Henry had come to see Vincent while Millie went out to talk to a travel agent. Not that she was definitely going to Wales. She just wanted to see about a ticket. Millie still wasn't telling him what to do, he had to say that. She had her opinion and she was letting him have his. "Looked at one way, Henry, he is *your* lizard," she'd said. "There's no way I'm saying that's not true. And in the end, I guess you have to decide."

But if Vincent stayed here, if Henry kept coming down and seeing Millie and hearing about Aelf and about the cave, it was going to get harder and harder not to just let her have it her way, Henry could see. And was that really fair? Millie was nicer than most people, but in the end what she was doing came to the same thing. Just like his mother and Dr. Ferguson, she was taking over. She was saying he ought to give up the most important thing he had; give up the chance to be a person who mattered; go back to being just that weird kid Henry Berg with the dope fiend father. He couldn't do that. Henry finally just felt it. He couldn't. Vincent was his and he was going to stay his. But he had to act fast.

He stood up and looked around for the box Millie had used to bring Vincent back from the university. It was under the kitchen table. Henry stuffed the lizard into it, threw in a handful of mealworms, and then called a taxi.

When Millie got back, nobody would be there but Jack. That was the only way. He shut the door and hurried down the steps to wait out front for the taxi. He and Vincent were heading for his grandparents' empty house on the lake. To the boathouse. The cab pulled up and he climbed in.

"Whatcha got in the box, little boy?" said a lady in tight pants and bright red lipstick who was already in the cab.

"A baby dragon," Henry said, feeling light-headed and relaxed because he had made up his mind—gotten past that miserable worrying.

"Really, you have got something alive in there," the lady said. "I hear it scratching around. Let's see."

"No," Henry said. "It's an iguana from Mexico, but I can't open the box. It might get out."

"Please don't," the lady said, with a shudder. "I never could see how people could fool around with those slippery things, snakes and all."

"You get all kinds, driving a cab," the driver said. "But not all that many lizards. You keep that top on, kid."

It was windy at the lake when Henry got out of the cab and headed for the boathouse; the lake was slapping up against the shore in a way it almost never did. Henry was starting to feel nervous, itchy, and miserable about what he was doing, and the slap, slap, slap of the water didn't help much.

"Good thing we're getting you inside, Vincent," he said, groping around under the back porch, where he knew his grandfather kept the extra boathouse key. "This wind could freeze you."

The boathouse was dark and empty. His grandfather didn't leave his boat there in the winter because he was afraid it might be stolen. There were some tools and ropes and cans of gasoline around, and piles of cushions and life preservers. Henry had figured he would improvise a cage at first, and then build something permanent when he had the time. There was a wooden box holding cushions and he dumped them out and laid one of the front porch screens across the top of it. Weighted down with some rocks and bricks from along the shore, it would keep Vincent secure and reasonably comfortable. It was dark in there, but Vincent liked the dark.

"See you soon, Vincent," Henry said, looking back toward the box in the corner, making sure everything was shipshape before he locked the door and headed home. It was a long walk and he had to make it by dinnertime to keep his mother from asking questions. "Back in a couple of days, Vincent," he said. "Don't stuff yourself on those hot dogs." He'd found out from Millie that Aelf liked meat, so he'd taken a few minutes to run out to the store down the road to buy a package of smoky links for Vincent. It was a special treat for him, in case he got lonely in the boathouse.

He'd taken care of everything, Henry thought, heading down the road toward town. Now everything was back on the track, proceeding according to plan. The only possible complication now was Millie, and what could she do? If she talked to his mother and Ferguson, she'd get herself in all kinds of trouble. After all, she was the one who took Vincent out of the lab, not Henry. Ferguson was still burned up.

about losing Vincent—he wouldn't listen to anything she said. And nobody was going to believe her dragon talk, not with Aelf dead. They'd say her mind was going. Old people and children, nobody believed either of them. That was what made his plan airtight. Now nobody would connect him with the dragon; his mother couldn't be after him to get rid of it, and Vincent would have time to develop all his amazing powers.

Maybe they could work out an act, Henry thought. Be on television together, do a few tricks, maybe go on talk shows and be interviewed. He would have to leave school. Go to one of those special classes he had read about in *TV Guide* that child actors go to. He would be on the road a lot. That would be educational, more than going to school. He'd *see* the products of New Zealand if he wanted to, not sit there with a blurry old ditto sheet, filling in the answers to a lot of dumb questions.

The only thing he wished now—he wished that Millie hadn't been so sure she was right. He wished he hadn't had to run off on her like that. Millie. She'd get so excited talking about Aelf, her glasses would slide down her nose and she'd be staring off over them, not even noticing. You could tell that she was seeing Aelf again, seeing the dragon cave, was looking off into the distance at pictures in her head almost the way Henry did when he thought of the river and of outer space in his room at night. Not many people did that—looked at mysteries that way, especially not many old ladies. But, say! It hit him. A great idea. When he and Vincent were rich and famous, he'd have lots of money he could give to Millie. She would have the chance to do everything she'd always wanted to—go around the world even. Then she'd see how right he'd been; then they could be friends again.

"That was the only way, Henry," she'd say. "Taking that lizard off that day. I was wrong to want to stop you."

"That's all right, Millie," he would answer. "You couldn't be sure how it would turn out." Henry hurried off down the road, almost running, feeling much better now that he had thought it out a little more.

Millie, when she got back from checking on her ticket, had a sinking feeling almost as soon as she opened the door. "Henry! Where are you?" She had known all along that the boy just wasn't seeing it the way she was. And she didn't blame him. He was too young to realize the risks, to see how dangerous and sad the situation could become. And he wanted that dragon for himself.

She looked around in the bedroom and the bathroom, but she knew neither Orm nor Henry would be there. She'd been taking a chance when she left them here, but she didn't know what else to do. She couldn't keep Henry away from Orm. He was involved as much as she was, and had as much right to decide what to do. There was something to be said for the idea that Orm belonged to him, Millie thought wearily, sinking down into her recliner. In a way it was a relief to think, "All right, let him worry about it now, I've done what I could."

If she could just get the memory of Aelf out of her mind,

forget about the way he thanked her for her help. "Aelf," she said, "I'll wait and see. If Henry has problems, he'll have to come to me. There's nobody else. And there is no way he won't have problems."

Saturday, just one week and a day since he and Millie had gotten Vincent back from Ferguson, Henry had fixed it so he could spend the whole afternoon out at the boathouse, working with the dragon. On his bike, he could get out there in twenty minutes. He told his mother he was going for a bike ride to look for fossils along the shore, for another science project.

Someday he would have to do something for a project in that class, Henry thought, pulling up beside the boathouse, or he would be in plenty of trouble. Make a mobile out of a coat hanger like that dumb Jodi across from him, or some stupid thing like that. Or, maybe, by the last week of school, Vincent would be ready to come to his science class. Maybe he'd have him trained by then. They could do some kind of simple act. Have everybody gasping, "What kind of lizard *is* that, Henry?"

Pulling off the screen and looking in the crate, Henry saw that Vincent was curled up, fast asleep. He slept through almost anything, Henry had noticed. That was a sign of a powerful animal, an animal that preys on others. Henry had read somewhere that rabbits and other helpless kinds of animals that had to worry about being eaten didn't sleep much. But lions and other meat-eating attack animals slept like logs for hours.

"Vincent!" Henry leaned over the crate to get his attention. Vincent's eyes blinked open, glowing dimly, then brighter. The dragon looked up, his attention caught by the key Henry had around his neck on a string, the key to his bike lock. He reached for it. He had an instinct to go for shiny things, Henry thought. Must be connected to the way dragons guarded treasure, jewels, gold.

"Keep away from that," Henry said. "It's mine." He looked around, wondering if his grandfather had left anything around that might make Vincent happy, make him feel he was guarding something. "How about this?" He shook a handful of brass screws and nuts into his palm and held them down for Vincent to see. In the beam of sunlight near the cage, the hardware gleamed almost like gold. Vincent's eyes lit up and glowed. He opened his mouth. A small flame, like a flower petal, licked along his teeth, just for a second. Henry drew back, startled, looking at the little curl of smoke, just a wisp, floating out of Vincent's mouth. He was so surprised that he drew his hand back, forgetting to give Vincent the brass screws.

The lizard rushed toward his hand in a fury, his eyes glowing, his foreclaws stretched out, the nails gleaming and sharp. Henry dropped the screws into the box hastily. Vincent scraped them into a pile and pushed them over to the side of the box, under a rag Henry had put there to keep him warm. Henry sat down beside the box, feeling a little shaken up.

He was going to have to think this thing through carefully. This dragon wasn't like a pet cat. He wasn't going to be a pet at all, that was never the idea. They were going to be partners. Equals. But Henry was going to do the planning, set up the acts. Teach Vincent how to act around people and so forth.

Rewards. That was probably the way to go about training him. Give him one of those screws every time he did something right. Henry decided, first of all, to work up some kind of trick connected with his breathing fire. That would certainly amaze everybody. There were piles of old newspapers over by the door. He went and got one and made a tiny torch by folding up a single sheet. He dragged over a bucket of sand that his grandfather kept in case of fire, so he could put out the newspaper torches. Then he got the jar of screws down and set to work. He wanted Vincent to blow fire onto his newspaper torch whenever he held up one of the screws and said, "Gold, Vincent, blow fire for gold."

With just one screw instead of a whole handful, Vincent was less excited and easier to work with. He didn't attack Henry's hand, and he watched and seemed to be trying to figure out what he was supposed to do. The third time Henry said it, Vincent blew a small flame right onto the newspaper.

"Great, Vincent, great!" Henry said and threw him the screw. He doused the fire with a handful of sand and tried again. After that, Vincent set fire to the torch perfectly three times in a row, collecting three screws and adding them to the pile under his rag. He understood the trick! This was easier than Henry had imagined.

Henry was just rolling up paper for one last torch when he heard the door open behind him. Turning quickly, he saw Mrs. Warren's Pekingese from down the way. He'd always hated that snub-faced, stuck-on-itself little dog. "Get out of here, Chien-Chien, you stupid moron!" He got up and picked up a broom to shake at him. Chien-Chien must have smelled Vincent. He was excited, and he was not paying any attention to Henry. Yapping his foolish head off, he started running around the boathouse, circling toward Vincent's box. "Out! Out!" Henry ran after him with the broom. The screen was off Vincent's box, Henry realized. Then Vincent climbed out and stood there looking fierce, as the dog circled him.

Henry started to panic. He had to catch that wretched mop of a dog. All he needed was for Vincent to kill it; he kept seeing that striped cat, its legs stretched out like sticks, dead at the river. "Get out of here! Go home!" he yelled. Chien-Chien, his orange fur standing on end, kept growling and making runs up at Vincent, then backing off again.

Henry dashed over and slammed the door, so that they wouldn't get out into the yard. Then he tried to intercept Vincent and grab him. The lizard was fast and dodged just out of his reach. Chien-Chien banged into a shelf and a lot of stuff fell onto the floor, almost hitting Vincent. Vincent reared up on his hind legs and breathed fire.

Henry's heart stopped beating. A gas can had fallen and spilled—the top must have been loose. There was a puddle of gasoline on the floor. Henry saw that, and he saw Vincent breathe fire, and for an instant he stood, frozen.

Flames burst out all over that end of the boathouse. Henry ran toward them and grabbed Vincent. Chien-Chien was already over by the door. As soon as Henry shoved it open, the dog took off, heading back home so fast he was a blur. Henry, desperate, rolled Vincent up in his sweater and dropped him in his bicycle basket. The fire was roaring in there. There was nothing he could do but get the fire department. He jumped on his bike and tore down the road to the corner near the highway. There was a pay phone there. He dropped in a dime and dialed O. "Fire!" he said. "Get the fire department." He gave the address, hung up, and sat in the booth, shaking. He had to get out of there; he couldn't be hanging around when the trucks got there. Vincent lay still, wrapped in his sweater. After checking him, Henry got back on his bike and took off toward town.

A half mile down the road there was an empty beach. Henry pulled in off the road and sat down against a tree. He had to get hold of himself and decide what to do. He checked Vincent in his bicycle basket. Curled up asleep. Just like nothing at all had happened. For a minute Henry started to hate the lizard. Burning down the boathouse, nearly killing all three of them, then peacefully snoozing away like nothing at all had happened. What kind of a monster was he? Then he remembered something Millie had said. "You can't start to think he's a person, Henry." He heard her voice saying it. "He belongs to a world of his own. You just can't expect him to do what you want him to."

Dumb. That was what Henry Berg was. Stupid. Warped. Weird. A nerd. A jerk. Henry sat and pulled up grass all around him and threw it into a pile. And now what could he do? He couldn't go back to Millie's after tricking her. And he couldn't take Vincent home. There was no way.

Suppose, he thought, suppose he just took Vincent out of his basket and left him here. Turned him loose? Wouldn't Vincent be happier that way? He could be free and do whatever he wanted. It wouldn't be Henry's fault whatever happened then. Probably he would just go off and live in the woods or something.

Henry stood up. He walked over to his bike and picked up Vincent. The sweater came loose and Vincent stuck his head out. He looked at Henry and his eyes glowed. Standing there, Henry remembered the day Vincent went wading in the river, how he had looked at him then. He remembered all the nights in his room, talking to him in the dark. He remembered the day Vincent had hatched, come uncurled on his bureau. "Damn!" he said. "Damn!" He wrapped Vincent back up, wheeled his bike out to the road, and started off again for town.

Millie was standing by her stove, stirring up a can of soup, when she heard them on the sidewalk down below. "Don't be silly," she said to herself, her heart skipping a beat. "Don't be silly; bicycles stop down there all the time." Then she heard steps coming up. She rushed to the door and opened it.

"I can't keep him," Henry said. "You were right. We have to get him back to Wales."

The poor boy looked pale and miserable. Something awful must have happened, Millie thought. "You're doing the decent thing, Henry," she said. "I really respect you for that."

TEN

DRAGON FIRE

Millie had read that getting animals into Britain was very difficult. There was a rule that you had to leave them in cages with some kind of customs officials for several months. Here was where being an old lady might be of some use, she'd told Henry. They'd be after flashy types, not somebody's ordinary old grandmother.

She and Henry had fixed up a small overnight case from the discount store to hold Vincent. They'd made breathing holes in it that didn't show, and fixed Vincent a bed inside. They put him in it for practice for several hours at a time before she left. He liked a dark, enclosed space anyway, and would sleep peacefully in there with no complaining and very little scrabbling around. Still, carrying him on to the plane, pushing the case under her seat, Millie gave a little shiver. She was a smuggler. Suppose she was caught sneaking this lizard in? All the way across the ocean, flying into the sunrise, her worries about the difficulties ahead kept her wide awake.

"Anything to declare?" The customs man at Gatwick Airport in London looked bored to death. Millie, her heart beating fast, couldn't say anything. She shook her head and walked past the barrier, on into the terminal. If Vincent had had any metal on him the bomb detection devices would have spotted him right away in Chicago, or even back in Oshkosh. If those attendants had been paying any attention, really watching that X-ray screen, they'd have seen something strange. She had passed three sets of people in badges, carrying a dragon in her bag. Now it was over. All she had in front of her was a bus to Wales and the end of her career as a mother to dragons.

Millie and Orm spent that day and night in London, resting up from the trip. "You look worn out, dearie," the maid at the bed-and-breakfast place said as Millie was going into her room, carrying the bag with Orm and another one with her clothes. "Let me help you with that." She reached for the bag with Orm.

"No!" Millie pulled back. She was so nervous, she was jumping out of her skin. She had to calm down. "No, thank you, I can manage." She gave a kind of weak smile to the maid, who shrugged her shoulders and looked insulted. She would have to leave her a nice tip to make up for it, Millie thought, as she sank onto the bed in the safety of her room. She got up and opened Orm's case. He was sleeping, but he woke up almost immediately, his eyes shining.

There was a largish closet, and Millie shut him up in there. Too bad she couldn't afford a private bathroom, she thought. He'd probably love the coolness of the tub after being so cramped. A picture of Aelf came to her mind, all the green coils of him in her bathtub. She was glad she had come, glad she and Henry had done this. "Take it easy in there, Orm," she said. "I'll go and get you some hamburger." She changed into her old walking shoes and went out to find a market.

The travel agent in Oshkosh had been puzzled about what she was doing, trying to find a place near the mountains in Wales. "The Welsh seacoast is really more attractive," the girl had said, "or the Scottish mountains."

"No, I'm just interested in the Welsh mountains," Millie said, leaning over and looking at the map. "Near the old King Arthur country. Not too far from the border. Here," she said pointing to some mountains called the Brecon Beacons. "I'd like to go there." It was partly guesswork, but from talking to Aelf she'd gathered that it was somewhere like that—isolated but not deserted, near people but apart from them—that the dragons had their secret caves.

"All right, I'll see about a room for you in Brecon, then," the girl had said, acting as if she still thought Millie was being foolish.

Pushing through the mobs of people in Victoria Coach Station, looking for the bus to Wales, Millie remembered the girl's doubts. She had no idea what she was getting into, and she was still feeling panicky when anyone bumped into

Orm's carrier. It was a long bus ride, though, and she had time to calm down, looking out the window at England, green and lovely. In the afternoon they came into the Cotswolds, a series of little villages made of honey-colored stone, and then they rolled across the border into Wales. There the country was wilder and there were fewer houses. More like Wisconsin, Millie thought.

Brecon turned out to be a small town with narrow, winding streets, all black and gray and white. There was a statue of the Duke of Wellington out in the square, and an old gray stone church opposite it. All the buses ground to a stop by the statue, and it was there that she and Orm would catch the sightseeing bus tomorrow that would take them out into the Beacons. That would be Orm's last ride of the trip, his home. She hoped. It was silly, Millie thought, to have been so sure that this was the place to come; Wales was a big place. Were there dragons in the hills everywhere or just in one or two places? "You've done what you could, Millie Levenson," she said to herself, "and that will have to be that."

The next day she hiked up the mountain with fifteen or twenty other tourists from the bus. "This one is called Penn Y Fann," the man walking along behind her said. "It's the highest peak in the Beacons." He was swinging a stick, and looked, obviously curious, at the little case Millie was carrying. Orm was inside it.

"I'd have settled for the second highest," she said, and moved over to sit on a rock beside the path. Partly she really did want to catch her breath, and partly she wanted the line of people from the bus to go on ahead of her, to give her a chance to do something with Orm. The man laughed and walked on. "I'll see you at the top," he called back.

Millie looked out over the grassy mountains, brown and golden in the sun. There was something strange and beautiful about the place. For one thing, after the line of people had passed, it was still. She sat and listened to the wind in the grass and to the tinkle of the sheep bells. There were no trees or bushes even, just waving grass—almost like the mountain's fur—all a lovely golden bronze in the sun. It was a landscape that seemed to breathe, to be alive itself, so many colors of gold and brown and bronze and almost lavender shimmering in the sun. She remembered Aelf's story about Grettir watching the tourists, hearing about the New World. Probably that day was just like today, tourists in a line trudging up the mountain, to eat sandwiches at the top and look back at the town, small and green from up here, with little trees and the winding Usk River off in the distance. The past didn't seem far away here; today could have been a day hundreds of years ago, or maybe hundreds of years in the future when Orm would be grown up.

Millie stood up and picked up the case. "Enough woolgathering," she said to herself sternly. "Millie Levenson, get going and get this over with." There wasn't any way to know where to leave him; one place looked just like another up here. She walked away from the path, tripping once or twice on the rough ground, and looked around her, feeling helpless.

A few more steps and the sun was behind the peak and

part of the grass was shaded. Or maybe it was just a cloud shadow, but it felt right. "There," she said, "in the shadows." She opened the case. Orm jumped out, and looked around, head up, his face quivering a little as if he were straining after something he heard or maybe smelled off in the distance. He started to run, parting the grass as he zigzagged through it. In a minute he was gone; he never looked back.

"Goodbye, Orm," Millie breathed. "Goodbye from me and Henry." Millie closed the case and walked back to the path. She walked the rest of the way to the top and sat down with the others.

"I thought maybe you'd dropped by the wayside," the man with the stick said. "I was about to organize a search party." He was an American and liked to talk; Millie sat and asked him questions about East Lansing, Michigan, where he came from. She felt numb, now that it was over.

Millie ate dinner late that night; it was ten o'clock by the time she finished. She was unlocking her door just as the hotel manager came by. "Mrs. Levenson," he said, "you're in luck. Have you looked out the window in the past few minutes?"

"No," Millie said, "why should I?"

"The lights are out," he said, a kind of excitement in his voice. "The brightest I've ever seen them."

"The lights?"

"In the sky. Red and green they are, all across the sky over the mountains. Take a look out your window. I'll show you." She opened her door and they walked over to the window. She caught her breath. The lights were so bright they reflected off the buildings; the old church across the way shimmered as if waves of clear green water were washing over it. Then the red lights were strongest, and waves of pink washed over the church. The sky flashed and flamed with the wonderful lights.

"What is it?" she gasped.

"Some people say it's a special kind of northern lights caused by peculiarities in the atmosphere over the mountains," he said.

"What do other people say?" she asked, sensing that he thought there was more to it.

"My grandfather," he said, "used to say it was dragon fire."

He and Millie stood and watched it, silent. After he turned and went about his business, she stayed there, washed by the waves of light, staring off at the dark peaks in the distance. After a half-hour or so, the lights stopped and Millie went to bed.

She slept better than she had for a month; it was nearly nine o'clock when she woke up. Still groggy, she reached for her watch on the nightstand. And nearly dropped it. What was that, sitting on the stand beside the water glass and her old Timex watch? She picked it up. It was heavy and cool in her hand, and shone with lights, the way the sky had the night before. "An emerald!" She stared. It *was* an emerald. Now she knew, beyond any doubt. Orm was home. Safe.

ELEVEN
HENRY BERG

Millie and Henry sat in her living room and looked at the emerald. Henry was holding it up to the light, turning it, watching the way it gleamed and flashed from down inside. "Dragon fire," he said. "That's what it makes me think of. Those lights you saw and what the man called them."

"I wish you could have seen them." Millie smiled at him. "If you could have come, seen those hills, you'd know we were right. It is the place for Orm. Nothing else would have been right."

"I know it," Henry said, putting the emerald down on Millie's table, "but I still miss Vincent."

"I brought that back for you," Millie said, pointing to the emerald.

"Me?" Henry said. "Oh, no, that wouldn't be fair. They

108

gave it to you. It was you that spent all your money getting there and went to all the trouble and everything."

"You gave up Vincent," Millie said. "And I had the trip to Wales, after all. It's yours. Don't argue about it, Henry. I mean it."

"Let's say it belongs to both of us," Henry said. "I'll keep it for a while and then you can. To remind us of Vincent and Aelf." He picked it up and put it in his pocket. He had gotten to know Millie well enough to know there was no use arguing with her about something like that. If she decided something was right, she did it.

And it would be nice to take the emerald home and put it on the table next to his bed, where Vincent's terrarium used to be. He would keep it in the egg pouch. Henry hurried home, the emerald in his pocket.

"Honestly, Henry, you are going to hypnotize yourself with that toy jewel," his mother said, laughing and turning to Dr. Ferguson. "Look at that, Jim. Where on earth do you suppose Henry comes up with these things? Strange, glowing lizards, funny pieces of glass. Most boys would settle for baseball cards or stamps or something!"

Dr. Ferguson walked over and picked up the emerald to examine it. For a minute he looked startled. Then he shook his head and laughed. "You could almost fool somebody with that thing, Henry. Whoever made it should have been just a little smarter, made it small enough to pass for a real emerald." He handed it back.

"I don't think anybody made it to fool people with," Henry said. "I think they just made it to look pretty." He put it down next to him and stretched out his legs, feeling lazy and comfortable. He could take it to a jeweler and have everybody staring at him in amazement. His mother and Dr. Ferguson would feel pretty foolish, knowing this was a real emerald worth half of Oshkosh. But Henry didn't feel like doing that.

Walking back from Millie's, he had thought that was what he would do. Rush in and knock them both over with it. But the thought didn't last. He saw that the emerald was a private thing—like Vincent was, like his friendship for Millie was. And he didn't need some huge jewel to make him feel like a person anyway. Protecting the dragons, knowing that he was the person who kept their secret, made him peaceful in a way he hadn't been before.

He didn't have crowds of people chasing after his autograph. And he had to admit, he would still like that—sweeping around in a limousine, having people gasp, "Isn't that Henry Berg?" at the sight of him. But Henry knew that he'd had the guts to take Vincent back to Millie, to admit he'd been wrong. If he hadn't, the dragons would be in danger; their secret would be threatened. "Henry Berg," he muttered, half out loud, twirling the emerald around and watching the lights in it. It was a name he'd gotten to like—the name of a person who stood up and did things and didn't hang back, worried about what everybody was thinking.

"Now he's talking to himself," his mother said, smiling down at him, running her hand over his hair.

"The sign of a first-rate intellect," Dr. Ferguson said. "All great men talk to themselves."

"I can believe it!" his mother said. "The author of the best science report in the seventh grade."

"The Oshkosh authority on reptiles," Dr. Ferguson said. "Ann told me about your paper, Henry. You should be proud. I'd like to see it."

"Yeah, thanks," Henry said, embarrassed. While Millie was in Wales he'd written up a long report on what he'd learned about reptiles in trying to classify Vincent. Mr. Haase had been so impressed he'd even called up Henry's mother to tell her how good it was.

"If you are that interested in reptiles, Henry," his mother said, looking a little guilty, "maybe you should get another one. Maybe I wasn't all that fair about the one you had. It was just that story you told—but let's forget it. It's true, I'm afraid of lizards. Creepy little slimy things." She shuddered. "I know it's silly, and I hate to admit it, but it's true. Get what you want, as long as it's not poisonous and you don't let it loose. And I won't have to pretend to think it's cute."

"I might, Mom. Thanks," Henry said. "But after Vincent other lizards seem kind of dull anyway. I've been thinking more about astronomy lately. Maybe doing some reports on that. What it's like on other planets—Jupiter and all."

"You know what, Henry," his mother said, looking pleased. "Your father had a telescope. *He* liked to look at the stars. Knew the names of all the constellations. I'll ask Grandad—I'm calling him tomorrow. The carpenter has finished rebuilding the boathouse—I promised to let him know. I'll ask him what became of the telescope. I'll bet he still has it!"

"That would be great," Henry said. "Thanks." He hated hearing about that boathouse. All this time, his mother had been going to all kinds of trouble, getting estimates, checking with insurance adjustors and carpenters, calling his grandfather. It made him feel awful, knowing it was his fault. He tried to tell himself it balanced out—they had blamed him for breaking the egg, which wasn't his fault. Now they had no way of knowing that burning down the boathouse had anything to do with him. He certainly wasn't going to tell them, but he did try extra hard to do things like the science report to make it up.

"Oh, and Henry," his mother said. "Don't worry about Grandad's egg. He was very understanding about that. I explained that it was an accident, and that you've been doing so well lately, and he said you shouldn't let it upset you. Everybody makes mistakes, he said to tell you."

"Okay," Henry said, squirming. "That's good."

"I will see about that telescope, son," she said again. "That's a promise."

Henry smiled at her. His father. He'd never thought much about what his father was interested in. It was startling, sort of a shock, to think of staring up at the stars through the telescope his father had used. Henry remembered that time so long ago, sitting high up in the tree, listening to his father sing. If his father were here now—alive—would Henry tell *him* about the emerald?

Henry looked into the jewel, spun it, and watched the lights flash. He might. He really might.

He put the emerald in the pouch and lay back on his bed the way he liked to when he imagined himself places. Henry didn't go diving down into the river, being a fish anymore. Nor, in spite of wanting the telescope, did he think all that much about space when he lay in his room at night. Now what he did was go off to Wales—to a cave somewhere in the hills.

There, on a stone ledge in the smoky dark, sometimes a light would flash, flames would dart, half-closed eyes would glow suddenly, sending beams to light up the gold and the jewels piled in heaps around the edges of the cave. Or to flash off the skin of Hrothan, the Old One, breathing in and out, the guardian of all the dragons, sleeping for centuries in the worn-away cup in the center of the cave.

There Henry saw a little dragon, less serious than the others, watching, learning what to do. Learning soon to fly, to talk. And probably thinking sometimes of him. Remembering Henry Berg and Oshkosh, Wisconsin.

Someday, Henry told himself, turning the emerald around and around over his head, someday he and Millie would go there. They would stand outside the cave and they would see Vincent again. Until then, though, it made him feel good to lie in his room in Oshkosh and know that they were there—the dragons—peaceful, living their lives. The way they were meant to.

MS READ-a-thon—
a simple way to start
youngsters reading

Boys and girls between 6 and 14 can join the MS READ-a-thon and help find a cure for Multiple Sclerosis by reading books. And they get two rewards—the enjoyment of reading, and the great feeling that comes from helping others.

Parents and educators: For complete information call your local MS chapter. Or mail the coupon below.

Kids can help, too!

- -

Mail to:
National Multiple Sclerosis Society
205 East 42nd Street
New York, N.Y. 10017
I would like more information about the MS READ-a-thon and how it can work in my area.

MS Mystery Sleuth ™

Name _____
(please print)
Address_____
City_____ State_____ Zip_____
Organization_____

1—80